RACHELLE MCKEOWN

Broken Hearts, Open Minds

First published by Rachelle McKeown 2021

Copyright © 2021 by Rachelle McKeown

All rights reserved. No part of this publication may be reproduced, stored or transmitted in any form or by any means, electronic, mechanical, photocopying, recording, scanning, or otherwise without written permission from the publisher. It is illegal to copy this book, post it to a website, or distribute it by any other means without permission.

This novel is a work of fiction. The names, locales, characters and incidents portrayed in it are the work of the author's imagination. Any references to real people, events, establishments, organizations, or locales are intended only to give the fiction a sense of reality and authenticity, and are used fictiously.

First edition

Cover art by Brittney Leach

This book was professionally typeset on Reedsy. Find out more at reedsy.com

For Aunt Laura

"All happy families are alike; each unhappy family is unhappy in its own way."

Leo Tolstoy, Anna Karenina

Contents

Prologue – September 21, 2012 — iii

I Part One

1	The Horrors of Halloween Week	3
2	Insomnia Runs in the Family	6
3	Costume Shopping	14
4	Dementia Day	32
5	The Anniversary Dinner	36
6	The Broken Heart	53
7	The Interview Aftermath	61
8	Secrets, Secrets Are No Fun	65

II Part Two

9	A Long Way From Where We Were	87
10	Lazy Sunday	96
11	Family Dinner	102
12	Slut Shaming	113
13	Chinese Finger Traps	132
14	When the Smoke Clears	162
15	The Divorce	184
16	Death and a Motel 8	194
17	Sweat and Tears	203
18	The Funeral	206
19	Giving Thanks	211
20	Christmas Eve	218

Afterword	232
Acknowledgements	234

Prologue- September 21, 2012

The last meal Nancy made before she tore her Achilles tendon was chicken parmesan. She stood at the counter, inhaling the smell coming from the oven behind her as she chopped up tomatoes for salad. She was so busy smiling to herself and playing music in her head as she cooked that she didn't even notice her husband slide around the counter and sneak up behind her. She jumped a bit when he wrapped his arms around her small waist. She turned around, startled.

"Don't do that!" she yelled at him, letting a giggle escape.

"I can't show my wife some love?" Frank asked, turning her around and smiling at her.

"Not when I have a knife in my hand," she replied, kissing him.

"Then put it down," he said, gently guiding her hand to set the knife down on the counter behind her. He pushed her hair behind her ears and smiled, revealing wrinkles around his mouth and eyes. She kissed him back and he picked her up. He gently placed her down on the counter. She carefully glanced over at the hot stove to her left before leaning in and kissing him.

"Be careful," she said, "I'm fragile."

"Don't worry," he responded, caressing her face with one hand. He gently lifted her up and centered her lithe figure between the sink and the stove.

"I would never hurt you," he whispered. They exchanged mumbled "I love you's" and continued kissing until their son, Teddy, walked into the room.

"Ewww, get a room you two!" he exclaimed.

Frank stopped kissing his wife and turned his head to glance at his son. "If you can't take the heat, get out of the kitchen," he said with a smirk.

"Ewww, stop it! Mom cooks our food on that counter!"

"Teddy, when you're married, you'll understand," his father said, his left hand on his wife's breast. He gave it one last squeeze and slipped his hand out from under her shirt. Teddy shook his head in response. He was fifteen and while thoughts of sex occasionally crossed his mind, he couldn't imagine himself doing the deed.

"Can you tell Ariana dinner will be ready in twenty minutes?" his mom asked, freeing herself from her husband's embrace and jumping down from the counter.

"Yeah," he said, turning to walk upstairs, "I think

she's doing homework."

He walked up to Ariana's cracked door and knocked gently. "Hey Ari, can I come in?" he asked.

"Sure," she replied.

Teddy stepped into the pristine room. Her bed was squarely situated alongside the back wall and her desk was centered in front of a large window on the adjacent wall. She had novels piled neatly on top of her desk, one of which she was engrossed in when Teddy walked in. Upon hearing him enter, she closed her book and turned sideways in her desk chair to face him.

"What's up?" she asked, looking directly at him.

"Not much. Dinner's gonna be ready soon." He shifted his weight from his left foot to his right.

"Mom and Dad were being gross downstairs," he said, trying to make conversation. He cringed as he realized his poor choice of topic.

"Were they kissing again?"

"Yeah," he said, hesitant to say anything more to his eleven-year-old sister.

"That's gross. Madeline Gregory kisses her eighth-grade boyfriend all the time. It's nasty. She's always talking about sex too."

"Do you even know what sex is?"

Ariana shifted in her seat and after a moment's pause, replied, "Yeah."

"Then what is it?" Teddy questioned, sensing her

hesitancy.

"It's when two people lie on top of each other" she said matter-of-factly.

He made the noise of a buzzer and said, "Try again."

"I don't know then. Natalie said that it's when a boy lies on top of you."

"I mean that's the general concept, but there's a lot more to it."

"Okay, what else is there?" Her face began to screw up as she tried to figure out what more could possibly be involved.

"I don't wanna tell you. You're my little sister. That's weird."

"You're not that much older. Just four years."

Teddy shot her a sideways glance, his eyebrows raised.

"Just tell me," she begged.

"Nah, I don't think so," Teddy said.

"Please! I'm gonna sound like an idiot if someone at school asks me and I don't know what it is."

"No, you won't. I didn't know what sex was in sixth grade. Everyone is just going off false information at that point. No one knows enough to question anything."

"Madeline Gregory does," Ariana protested.

"Madeline Gregory is a slut," Teddy said, "I heard she had sex with a kid in my grade before she got with her new boyfriend."

"What's a slut?"

Teddy sighed.

"A girl who has sex with a lot of different people."

"How does sex make you a slut?" she asked, still searching for the definition of sex and hoping to better define "slut" in the process.

"Ask me in a few years," Teddy responded. "Just promise me you won't have sex with anyone."

"I promise," she said as if she were making an oath.

I

Part One

Part One

1

The Horrors of Halloween Week

"How was your day at work?" Frank asked Nancy as he set his briefcase down by the basement stairs. He sat down at the kitchen table to take off his shoes and noticed that Nancy was forcefully cutting up carrots in the kitchen.

"Geez it sounds like you're trying to kill someone over there," he said, dropping his shoes. He stood up and wandered over to the counter in the middle of their kitchen. He stood opposite her and watched her slam the knife down across three carrot tops.

"That's 'cause I want to" she said, not bothering to look up.

"That's not good. What's up?" He frowned, bracing himself for the answer.

She dropped the knife on the cutting board and raised her face to reveal tear stained cheeks.

"My boss is driving me nuts. He gives me a new task every ten minutes even though most tasks require at least 20 minutes. I get halfway done and he interrupts me for something new. I can't do it anymore."

"Aren't you just a receptionist?"

"I'm practically the man's personal assistant with the number of clients he has," she responded, putting her hands in her face and trying to muffle her tears.

Sensing that he was supposed to do something, Frank walked around the counter and hugged her. She started crying again, her tears falling on his blue blazer. He could feel her tears staining his clothes and pulled away. He readjusted his suit, then laid a hand on her shoulder.

"It'll be okay," he reassured her, "Why don't you talk to him about it?"

"I'm scared he will fire me if I try to confront him," she responded between sobs.

"Then you should quit before you get fired," Frank responded logically.

"But what am I going to do?"

"You'll find something," he said, his voice dropping an octave. "And if you don't, then don't worry. Teddy isn't going to college any time soon. We just have to worry about paying for Ariana's tuition. I can take care of it."

"But I don't want to put that pressure on you."

"Don't worry about it," he said with a tight-lipped smile. He stepped backwards and started towards the stairs, mumbling something incoherent under his breath as he walked away.

"Okay," she said, returning to her cutting board. "Easier said than done," she mumbled to herself. The sound of her furious cutting lasted for the next hour.

2

Insomnia Runs in the Family

The house was eerily quiet when Nancy came down stairs at midnight the next night. She usually didn't have problems with falling asleep, but she'd been restless the previous night as well because she was so stressed about quitting her job. She had started looking for jobs online after she had finished cooking the previous night and was realizing how hard it was to find something new at her age. It didn't help that her younger self had decided that history would be an appropriate back-up plan if her dance career failed. Now she was realizing that unless if she wanted to go back to school in some capacity, she would be doomed to any job description that simply required a four-year degree. She sighed, remembering the night she and Frank had met.

It was her senior year at Weslyean, a few months

before she had graduated and had been accepted into a local dance company. She had been living with her parents in Derby and Frank had just enrolled in Yale's Law School, so they frequented the same bars at night. As she made herself a bowl of cereal, she couldn't help but remember the day they first met.

They had met at Brother Jimmy's, a local bar that was known for its club scene despite its lack of a large dance floor. Frank had been drinking alone at the bar and she had been ordering drinks with a friend. He had offered to buy her a drink and she had accepted. She was used to men hitting on her and grabbing her ass without permission, so the fact that he bought her a drink first set him apart from the men she was used to. He motioned for her to sit down next to him at the bar as she waited for her drink and began talking to her.

"So, what do you do for a living?" he asked, smiling with his eyes as well as his teeth.

"Nothing yet," she laughed nervously, "I'm in my last semester at Weslyean right now."

"Ah, you're making me feel like an old fart. I just started law school over at Yale," he said, laughing. He had somehow managed to smile and sip his drink at the same time. She remembered feeling butterflies when he had looked at her like that.

"Damn, law school at Yale? That sounds intense. You must be really smart though."

He smiled knowingly. "Yeah," he said, taking another sip of his drink. "So what are you doing over at Weslyean?"

"Dancing," she said, sipping the drink he had bought her and watching skepticism dance across his face.

"My dance teacher said that if I really want to launch a career, I need to get exposure to people in the industry and that the best way to start networking is by getting a degree." She paused and he sipped his drink slowly.

"I'm double-majoring in history," she added.

The hesitation left his face as quickly as it had settled in. "Ah, so I'll see you on Broadway soon?" he asked, winking at her. She smiled sheepishly.

"I hope," she said.

"If you don't mind me asking, how old are you?" He rested his arm on the table and stared intently into her eyes.

Taken aback by the stare, she had looked away and glanced down at her drink. She took another swig before saying anything.

"No, it's fine. I'm twenty-one," she responded, casting a sideways glance at her friend, who was still waiting on her own drink.

"Really? I'm twenty-five," he said. She blushed back at him, clearly embarrassed. He smiled and said, "You look so young. I almost wondered if you got in here with a fake."

Nancy blushed more. "Yeah, I know I have a baby face."

"Not a baby face, a beautiful face. Would you care to dance with me?"

She glanced at her friend, who was now brandishing a drink and watching Nancy and Frank talk with a smirk on her face. Her friend winked at her and motioned towards a cute guy on the other side of the bar. "Well, I am a dancer," Nancy said.

Nancy's reverie was interrupted when she heard the garage door. Teddy walked through the basement door a few minutes after it shut and Nancy was rudely reminded of what had changed: having two kids and a career-ending injury. It didn't help that lately her husband's charm only seemed to be put to use in the courtroom and not to get her into the bedroom.

"Hey Mom," he said in a daze.

"Hi," she said solemnly, trying to push her ugly thoughts away. When she finally convinced herself not to dwell on the past and instead focus on the present, she realized that her son was high and sighed to herself in defeat. This was the third night in a row that he had come in late this week and she was sick of watching him smoke his nights away. Her eyes narrowed in on Teddy as he stood by the open pantry door and began shoveling chips into his mouth. He caught her gaze, lowered his eyes, and started towards the stairs with a bag of chips, leaving a trail of crumbs on the floor. She called out to him and asked him to sit down. He grudgingly turned around and walked over. He sat down at the table and she began her interrogation.

"Where were you?" she asked.

"At Dexter's," Teddy responded with his mouth full. Pieces of chip stuck to his lips.

"What were you guys doing so late?"

"Just hanging out."

"Really? You weren't doing anything else?"

"No Mom, what do you think I was doing?"

Nancy's eyes narrowed even more, focusing in on Teddy's bloodshot eyes. She held him in this stare for a whole minute, hoping that it alone would make Teddy confess. It used to work wonders on her kids when they were children. She was losing her effect though; Teddy wasn't saying anything.

"Smoking weed" she responded firmly.

"How? I don't have any. You would smell it."

"Not necessarily," she said, choosing her words carefully. Her son didn't need to know that she had smoked a few times herself. "There are ways to hide it."

"Search me," he said, shoving another handful of chips into his mouth. He spread his arms wide, waiting for a pat down.

"Okay, so you're smart enough to at least leave it

at Dexter's? Because you know your father would lose it if he found it in this house."

Teddy shifted in his seat at the thought of his dad discovering the stash he had in his sock drawer.

"Teddy, I'm not stupid. I know that's all you've been doing since high school and it's gotten worse since you dropped out of UNH and lost your job. I don't like it, but I know I can't stop you from doing it. I want you to be honest with me though. So I'm going to ask one more time. Were you and Dexter smoking tonight?"

"No," Teddy said, grabbing more chips.

Nancy leaned back in her seat and decided to try a different technique. "I'm not going to tell your father because I know he's already screamed at you so many times about it," she said.

"There's nothing to tell, Mom," Teddy said, spitting bits of chewed chips all over the kitchen table.

"Ugh, Teddy, that's disgusting" she said, standing up and instinctively heading towards the kitchen to grab paper towels. "Clean that up."

Instead of listening to his mother, Teddy got up, grabbed his bag of chips, and started upstairs to his room, exhausted by both his high and his mother. Nancy followed him towards the stairs and firmly whispered, "Clean that up. I've cleaned up after you your whole life. You're twenty-one now. It's not my job anymore."

"Goodnight, Mom."

"Teddy, I swear to God, if you don't wipe it up, I will, and then I'll smear it all over you in your sleep."

Teddy's bloodshot eyes grew to twice their size and he swiveled around to face his mother.

"You wouldn't," he said, glancing at her stern face. Nancy raised one eyebrow in reply.

"Fine," he said, and passed her on his way back downstairs. Nancy smiled to herself as she walked up the stairs.

She entered her room and turned on the light to get ready for bed. Frank had told her he was working late again, but she had a sneaking suspicion that he wasn't actually working, as he had come home smelling like scotch almost every time he used that excuse in the past month. She had been considering confronting him for the past two weeks but every time she tried, the doubt the maybe all their problems were in her head prevented her from saying anything.

The more she thought about Frank, the more she was reminded of the way their marriage used to be. She knew her body wasn't the same — she had gained a substantial amount of weight due to her injury — but she didn't think that was entirely to blame for their lack of a relationship.

As she thought back, she realized it had all started after they got settled into married life. That was when she had begun to notice his general lack of compassion and weak attempts to make up for it. As the years went on, the good days became harder to come by. She watched him slowly become an unfamiliar person but tried to pretend everything was okay for the sake of her kids. She hadn't wanted to uproot them by getting a divorce and moving them.

And look where that's gotten Teddy, she thought, *he'd probably have been better off if I had gotten divorced.* She wanted to cry as she wondered how different their lives would be if she had stood up for herself years ago. A little voice in the back of her head told her that it wasn't too late, but she wasn't so sure. She cried as she brushed her teeth in the master bathroom and went to bed with a twinge of guilt and a general feeling of inferiority. Even her cat, Tux, who usually comforted her when she was upset, was too busy napping in her closet to hear the sound of her sobs.

3

Costume Shopping

Nancy used to love brushing Ariana's hair when she was little because it was the only time she could ever get her to sit still. Her long black hair felt like silk and Nancy used to braid it all the time. Now she longed to touch it as she watched it fall around Ariana's face while she danced around the living room. Nancy used to take her to dance classes all the time when she was younger in hopes that her daughter would fall in love with dance as she had. She had never expected her to have stuck with it through high school, but her daughter was quite the ballerina. She had fallen in love with her tutu as a little girl and used to refuse to take it off. Nancy remembered Ariana's first dance recital when she was four, her hair piled high in a bun on the top of her head and her stomach ever so slightly protruding over the edge of her tutu. She tried to place that little girl in her mind as she watched Ariana dance around the living room in a tank top and sweatpants, her long hair hanging free and flailing all over the place. She had the sudden realization that Ariana wasn't a child anymore and felt a rush of emotion wash over her. Nancy put her hand over her mouth to conceal her wavering lip and waited for the song to end before interrupting.

"Great job!" she exclaimed, "Do you feel ready for your recital next week?"

"Ehh, I still need to work on my triple pirouette. I can get it most of the time but I'm not 100% confident yet. It's annoying because I've been working on it for so long."

"I'm sure you'll be fine. Did you want to head to the mall now?"

"Yeah, just let me do one more run-through first."

Nancy looked on at her daughter nostalgically. She missed being able to dance herself but was glad her daughter was able to still enjoy it. She remembered the days before she tore her Achilles tendon and was able to train. She missed performing with the company, even if they didn't travel far or often. She glanced down at her protruding stomach and touched her hands to her hulking thighs. *I couldn't even go back to teach there looking like this*, she thought. She sighed heavily. She knew she would never again be able to move the way Ariana could if she tried, but watching her daughter dance stirred a dormant desire in her. She walked over to the kitchen counter and jotted two more items down on a piece of paper before heading to the bathroom.

<u>To-Do</u>
Get milk and eggs
Find Teddy's house keys
Call Dr. Melnyk
Look into Zumba classes

Ariana finished her routine and walked over to the counter to grab a glass of water. She glanced at Nancy's to-do list and put her water down.

"Mom, who's Dr. Melnyk? And what's this thing about Zumba?"

"She's my new doctor," Nancy responded, yelling from hallway outside the bathroom.

"And I think it would be good for me to start dancing again," she said as she entered the kitchen again.

"Really?" Ariana asked, "Why now?"

Nancy paused, unsure of exactly why the thought had hit her at this precise moment in time. It was, after all, not the first time she had watched Ariana dance since her injury, yet something about this moment was different.

"Because I miss it," she said. *Because I'm remembering what makes me happy*, she thought to herself as she walked over to the side table by the basement door and grabbed the car keys. Ariana followed and grabbed a sweatshirt that was hanging over a kitchen chair. They left for the mall and made some small talk, but fell silent within the first five minutes of the ride.

Ariana didn't want to risk talking too much and mentioning an upcoming Halloween party to her mother, but at the same time, felt the silence itself might be perceived as suspicious. She broke the silence by mentioning that she wanted to get a costume so that she could join her friend, Kelsey, at a small get together she was having next Friday night. Explaining why they were celebrating the holiday ten days late required her to lie to her mom that Kelsey and her family were out of town this weekend, so they were pushing their Halloween celebration back. In reality, Bryce, the one hosting the party, had messed up the dates his parents would be out of town, so his Halloween party was delayed until the second weekend of November. Dan, Ariana's boyfriend, had complained about why they still had to dress up if the party was no longer on Halloween, but Bryce had insisted that most people had already bought costumes and that they might as well wear them. Ariana, who hadn't bought a costume in advance of the party, had argued that Dan could buy one on Halloween and probably pay half of what he normally would, like she was planning on doing.

Ariana felt a sigh of relief when her mother continued the conversation by asking her questions about a potential costume and not asking too many questions about the party. She tried to contain her excitement that her lie had worked and that she was finally going to a real high school party. Bryce's party was the first one she'd ever been invited to and it was all because her and her friend Kelsey were both dating school athletes. She was just beginning to become friends with some of Dan's friends who were cheerleaders, Marcy and Anna, and hoped that this party would seal her status as one of the popular people in school. The girls had already bonded over participating in performance-based sports, and had even offered to teach Ariana tumbling if she decided she wanted to pursue cheerleading in college instead of dance.

Nancy used her daughter's excitement to fuel some of her own. After the previous night, she was ready to hit the reset button and figured that the best way to start was by shopping for some new clothes. As her and Ariana reached the conclusion that Ariana should either be a boxer or Rosie the Riveter for Halloween, Nancy pulled into the parking lot and the two women got out of the car.

As they walked through the aisle of Halloween costumes, Nancy was reminded of how revealing most of the costumes were and remembered that her daughter was no longer five, but seventeen, and was fast approaching the age where she would want to dress as something half naked for Halloween. Ariana walked ahead into the next aisle, popped her head around the corner, and waved her mother over. She brought her mom to the boxer outfit, which came with a robe, a sports bra, spandex shorts, and boxing gloves. Nancy took one look at the model on the front of the package and shook her head.

"This is what they call a costume? No, that's a waste of money. $50 to dress you up as someone half-naked?"

"But mom, it's cute," Ariana pleaded, trying not to whine. "And it's marked down. It was $75 before."

"It's slutty and overpriced," Nancy said, looking away from the costume and turning her gaze towards her daughter. "Do you really want to be one of those girls that leaves nothing to the imagination?"

"That's not slutty! Everything important is covered okay? Girls work out in the gym in those clothes."

"Do those girls have ringworm?" Nancy retorted.

Ariana rolled her eyes. "Ugh. Mom, Marcy and Anna are going as a devil and an angel and I highly doubt their boobs will even be in their costumes."

"And what's Kelsey wearing?" Nancy asked with pursed lips.

"She's gonna be a maid," Ariana said staunchly, pointing at a maid's costume that wasn't too far away. Nancy saw the short skirt and the revealing neckline and considered that there might be more important battles to fight in the near future.

Nancy rolled her eyes. "Okay, fine, but I'm not paying $50 when you already have half of the costume at home. If you can find the robe and boxing gloves separately, I'll pay for those. And get real gloves because I'd like to use them when you're done with them."

"But mom, they're not going to sell just the robe and gloves. Also, since when do you box?"

"Well, never, but I might like to try it," Nancy responded. Ariana sighed in defeat and the two women left the store. They turned right out of the party store and walked in silence for a bit, Ariana trying to figure out a way to complete her Halloween costume and Nancy trying to remember what she came to the mall for in the first place. They passed a jewelry store on their left, a phone store on their right, and a small boutique-like store next to the phone store. Ariana, who was looking around for inspiration, suddenly spotted a sport store a few stores ahead.

"Mom, they might have gloves in there," she said, pointing. Nancy looked up and saw the sport store.

"Okay," she said. Ariana sped up in her excitement

and Nancy tried to match her pace. She felt her heart lurch in her chest from the sudden increase of movement and hung back, breathless from the pressure in her chest.

"I'll meet you in there," she yelled ahead, spotting a bathroom on her right. "I need to go to the bathroom," she said. Ariana, who had whipped her head around at the sound of her mom's voice, nodded and proceeded towards the store.

Once Nancy got into the bathroom and managed to catch her breath, she called Dr. Melnyk, the cardiologist her doctor had referred her to. The receptionist initially told her the next available appointment was in a month's time, but when Nancy explained the sudden pressure she had felt in her chest, the receptionist managed to squeeze her in within the next week. Once they had set the appointment, Nancy hung up and put her phone in the purse that she always slung over her left arm.

She fixed her hair in the mirror and realized that a younger version of herself wouldn't recognize who she was now. It wasn't just her weight; it was her slumped posture, her thinning mousy hair, and the same jeans and top that she wore almost every time she left the house outside of work. She suddenly wished she could throw all her clothes away and dye her hair. She wasn't one for rash decisions though, so she tried to correct the only thing she could in the moment: her posture. She tried to walk out of the bathroom standing taller than she went in. *Although buying new clothes can't hurt,* she thought to herself as she walked into the sports store.

She quickly found Ariana among the athletic leggings rack and noticed a pair of boxing gloves in her hand.

"So you found half of it," Nancy said, glancing at the gloves.

"Yeah. I don't think I'm gonna find a robe in here though. I was thinking Victoria's Secret might have one."

Nancy raised her eyebrows. Not only did she not want her daughter wearing anything that could be used as lingerie to a party, but she also hadn't been in Victoria's Secret since she was fifty pounds lighter. She almost audibly shuddered at the thought of having to enter the store.

"Well why don't I browse a bit here and buy the gloves for you while you run to Victoria's Secret?" she said, her fear of the store overcoming her fear of her daughter's sensuality.

"Where is this coming from?" she muttered to herself after Ariana traipsed out of earshot. She tried to remember when her daughter had become a teenager as she mindlessly browsed through leggings, but couldn't seem to remember a pinnacle moment. Sure, Ariana was occasionally moody and would lash out on her father, but Nancy considered that normal given that her husband wasn't the easiest person to get along with.

She angrily pushed a pair of leggings aside at the thought of Frank, wishing she could push him out of her life so easily. She tried to remind herself that she was here with Ariana, and then her mind wandered to what exactly Ariana was up to. She had a sneaking suspicion that this sudden change had something to do with her boyfriend, who seemed like a stereotypical jock. Nancy had only met him once after a game, but had disliked him almost immediately. She had quickly picked up on his thin veneer of charm that disguised his arrogance (he had almost reminded her of a younger version of Frank), but she had kept her thoughts to herself for the sake of preserving her relationship with her daughter. She suddenly wondered if her daughter was having sex and tried to remember if she had ever talked to Ariana about being safe.

Worried that she had missed a crucial part of parenting, she moved onto the adjacent rack of long sleeve shirts. A long sleeve pink shirt caught her eye and distracted her from her thoughts. She held it up to her body, trying to envision herself in it. It looked like it fit, but instead of trying it on, she kept browsing. She then found a teal shirt that was similar in size, but slightly different in style. She piled that shirt on top of the pink shirt was already hanging over her left arm and circled back to the rack of leggings. She quickly found a grey pair in what looked like her size and checked out with all four items. As she stood at the cash register, she found herself unsure of why exactly she had picked out the clothes she had, but didn't regret it. *If I buy them, then I have to wear them*, she told herself, glancing down at the boxing gloves she planned on using once Ariana was done with them. She had never taken a kick boxing class before, but was sure that she had enough anger to unleash on a bag if she could find one. She wasn't sure why the thought of working out hadn't occurred to her before. Maybe it was because of her heart's physical and metaphorical protests against the way she was living her life.

Right as Nancy walked out of the store, Ariana texted her that she was leaving Victoria's Secret. Nancy texted her that she was going to sit down, and they met at a bench in the middle of the mall.

"Did you get your robe?" Nancy asked, scared to know what else was hiding in her daughter's shopping bag.

"Yep," she beamed, "And they had a sale on bras, so I got two. What did you get?" she asked, glancing at Nancy's rather large bag.

"I got a couple shirts and some leggings. They should be good for walking in the cold."

"That's good," Ariana said, although it was hard for her to hide the puzzled expression on her face. Her mother hadn't worked out in years, yet she had suddenly expressed interest in Zumba, boxing, and walking all in the same day. Ariana had a sneaking feeling that her mother wasn't giving her the whole story but she was glad that her mother wanted to be healthy, so she tried to smile. Nancy wasn't convinced though, and frowned in response.

"I'm sorry, I didn't mean that to come out weird. I'm glad you want to exercise," Ariana said, hoping she had recovered well. The two women hugged and continued shopping, Nancy trying to shake the thought of her daughter having sex and Ariana trying to not to think about why her mom was suddenly hell bent on losing weight. She had seen that her mother had written down making a call to a doctor on her to-do list and debated asking about it, but decided she didn't want to know the answer just yet.

* * *

As Ariana and Nancy shopped, Teddy was lying on his bed, waiting for a text from his friend, Dexter. He and Dexter had met when Dexter had moved to town during their sophomore year of high school. They had met in history class, where they had bonded over making fun of their teacher for his mustache and occasional twitch. Teddy didn't really think twice about seriously befriending Dexter at first though because Frank had taught Teddy to view people like Dexter as losers. When Teddy's grades started making him feel like a loser though, Dexter's care-free life style seemed much more appealing than his strict regimen of homework and soccer practice. One day, Teddy and Dexter started talking about grades and Dexter told him not to worry so much.

"Ten years down the road, no one's gonna care if you flunked AP Gov in high school," Dexter had said. Teddy had put that in Dexter's pipe, smoked it, and decided that Dexter was right. He had the sudden realization that he was on the fast track to becoming his father and the thought terrified him. He had felt himself sink into Dexter's couch and let relax himself for the first time in years.

Now he and Dexter smoked almost every day. In high school, it had been a fun game of sneaking off during their shared study hall to do so, but now it was two grown, unemployed men smoking in Dexter's basement. If Dexter's parents were irked by this behavior, they avoided showing it when Teddy was around; they even jokingly asked their son for a hit every so often in Teddy's presence.

As Teddy waited for Dexter to respond, he found himself wishing he had Dexter's parents. They always welcomed him with a smile even though he came over so frequently. He knew that might be because he had over-exaggerated the issues he had with his dad, but he wasn't going to complain about their sympathy. Regardless of the severity of the situation, being around his father was unbearable. Not only was he always casting disappointed looks at Teddy when they were in the house at the same time, but he also screamed at him every time he came home from work angry. Teddy didn't want to hear about how he was a failure because he wasn't like his father. He anxiously checked his phone to see if Dexter had gotten back to him about what time he could come over. The lack of notifications aggravated him and he threw his phone across the room.

Suddenly, he heard the garage door open. He got up from his bed and looked out the adjacent window. "Shit," he whispered as he watched his dad's car pull in. He walked across the room and picked up his phone. Still nothing from Dexter. He plopped down on his bed, taking his phone with him. He scrolled through Facebook until he saw a text from Dexter saying that he could come over at seven. Teddy sighed back onto his bed. He still had two hours to kill and he knew that he was being excluded from dinner at Dexter's. He began weighing his options, neither of which were appealing. He didn't want to go downstairs and scrounge together food for dinner, but he also didn't want to pay for food, especially since he was in month two of unemployment. He hadn't started looking for anything new since he had been laid off two months ago, which angered his father even more. He procrastinated on Facebook for about an hour and tried to convince himself that he wasn't hungry. By the time six o'clock rolled around though, his stomach was growling to the point where he could no longer ignore it. He picked himself up off the bed, grabbed his keys off his bureau, threw on a blue hoodie that was lying on his floor, and sauntered downstairs. He wore the hood over his shaggy brown hair as if it could shield him from the wrath of his father.

He found that Ariana and his mother had since gotten home from the mall and saw Ariana doing homework at the kitchen table. His dad had settled himself into the living room couch and was watching TV. Frank looked like he had nodded off, so Teddy quietly raided the fridge. The only snacks he saw were yogurt and cheese. Unsatisfied with his options, he walked toward the pantry and proceeded to raid it. He found the same bag of chips he had opened the other night and started munching.

"Hey Teddy," Ariana said, startling him. He dropped the bag of chips in his hand.

"Hey, what's up?" he said, bending down to pick up the chips and walking towards the kitchen table.

Ariana put her pencil down and directed her full

attention towards Teddy even though he was still a few yards away from her.

"Oh, not much. Haven't seen you in a while though."

"Yeah, sorry about that," Teddy said quietly, nodding towards his dad.

"You know, it might not be so bad if you bothered to show up for dinner every now and then," she harshly whispered.

"You don't understand," he said.

"Oh, but I do. He does the same thing to me now. 'Ariana, how are your grades? Are you going for extra help in math? Have you looked into any pre-law programs lately?' I want to punch the man in the face too but I suck it up."

"That's not even scratching the surface," he said, glancing over at their father and shoveling another handful of chips into his mouth.

Their father stirred on the couch and woke himself up. His vision settled in on Teddy, and the memory of his son faded back to him.

"Teddy, what are you doing here?" he asked sleepily, slowly getting up and making his way towards the kitchen.

"I'm just grabbing a snack before I go to Dexter's," he said, shoving a handful of potato chips into his mouth. He stood up and faced his father instinctively, preparing for a fight. Frank walked towards the fridge and grabbed a glass of scotch. He finished the glass in two swigs, set it down on the counter, and walked towards the kitchen table.

"Why aren't you staying for dinner?" Frank said, leaning in towards Teddy. Teddy backed away from the smell of the scotch on his breath. He had a feeling that the drink Frank had just finished wasn't his first one of the night.

"Is mom even cooking?"

"No, she ran to get take out. Panera, I think." Ariana said.

"Okay, so what's the point in me staying for dinner?" he said, glaring at his father as he shoveled another handful of chips into his mouth.

"Because the only thing I ever see you eat is chips," Ariana chimed in, "Have you even eaten a real meal in the past three days?"

Teddy paused to think for a second, but was cut off by his father, who was remembering why he was confronting his son.

"The point is you should want to eat dinner with your family," Frank said, raising his voice.

"'Family?' Do we have to pretend we all like each other?"

Ariana deflated and turned back to her homework, half-listening to her father and Teddy as she struggled through precalculus.

"We all like each other!" Frank yelled, his face

turning red with alcohol and rage.

"Since when? We haven't had a real conversation since I quit soccer six years ago."

Frank didn't know how to respond, so he slammed his fist down on the table. Ariana flinched but pretended to focus on her homework.

"I didn't realize that this is what love looks like," he said, gesturing at Frank with his hands. "Have you ever thought that this shit is the reason I'm never home? I'm going to Dexter's."

Teddy said goodbye to Ariana and walked out of the house. Frank shook his head, walked to the liquor cabinet, poured himself some more scotch, and retreated back to the living room.

4

Dementia Day

On Sunday morning, Frank made himself some coffee with a generous portion of Bailey's. Nancy gave him a judgmental stare as he filled half his travel mug with alcohol.

"You're going to see your dad with that?" she asked.

"Yeah," he said, popping a lid onto his mug. "How else am I supposed to get through the visit?"

"Can't you get pulled over for that?" Ariana interjected, overhearing their conversation from the kitchen table.

"No one's going to pull me over," Frank said. Ariana and her mother exchanged troubled looks as Frank popped the lid on his mug.

"Do you want any breakfast first? I'm about to make some eggs," Nancy asked.

"No," Frank said, grabbing a light jacket from the

closet and grabbing his keys from the counter. "I'll be back in about two hours," he said, not bothering to say goodbye.

Half an hour later, he found himself meandering through the halls of the nursing home, looking for his father. Finally, he found him in one of the open-air lounges staring at a dark television with two other old men.

"Hey Dad, how's it going?" Frank said, sitting down next to his father. The other two old men sitting near him turned to look at Frank and then turned their attention back to the television as if there was an entertaining program on. His father raised his right hand in half a wave and parted his lips to speak.

"Those things over there, the frisbees, they're–!" he trailed off in a Ukrainian accent, his laughter interrupting his thought. He was pointing at the blank TV screen.

"Yeah, they're something else, aren't they?" Frank said. *Are they sure he has dementia and that he's not just senile?* he wondered.

"Yah, yah," his father said, leaning back into the couch he was sitting on.

"Did you eat yet?" Frank asked, trying to make conversation. He knew that his father wasn't particularly lucid today, but he didn't know what else to say.

"You see 'im over there?" his father responded, leaning forwards in his seat and pointing towards a male aide in the hallway outside of the lounge.

"Yeah," Frank said, glad that his dad was able to string a sentence together but also unsure of where the conversation was going.

"He sends 'em up there," he said, pointing up towards the ceiling. "I wanna go."

You and me both, Frank thought to himself. "Yeah, you wanna go?" he asked.

"Tak," his father said, slipping into Ukranian. He leaned back in his chair again and Frank sighed. The father he had known had become completely unrecognizable and he wasn't sure if that was a good thing or a bad thing. A group of aides interrupted them for breakfast and brought everyone back to their respective rooms for meal time. Frank glanced around at the blank walls, contemplating how bleak old age seemed. The two men sat in silence as Yosyp ate breakfast. Frank turned the TV on to drown out the silence and left shortly after breakfast was over. As he drove home, he remembered the strict man his father used to be and recalled getting punished for not doing well in school.

"Education is key to success," his father had yelled in his accented English. "You must do well in school to get good job and pay bills."

He recalled nights of sitting in the dark because his

father hadn't made enough money at the factory to cover the electricity bill. "You either eat in darkness or starve in light," his mother had told him when he had complained about the power being out for the third day in a row. He had eaten his canned food reluctantly and had solemnly sworn to himself that he would do well in school, not to please his father, but so that he would never have to live like his father. He was old enough to know that other kids in his class didn't go days without electricity. His sister, Lisa, had been luckier than him. She was born after the factory his father worked for had unionized and refused to believe Frank's stories of sitting in darkness for days on end.

5

The Anniversary Dinner

Frank sat at his desk, fingering his wedding band. He glanced over the pictures of his wife and kids on his desk as if they were insignificant. He looked down at his phone at his wife's "Happy Anniversary!" text but he didn't look very happy. His face seemed to be drawn into a permanent frown and his eyes were tired. He was exhausted from work and didn't have energy for his wife.

It wasn't as though she was awful. She made him dinner and made love to him occasionally, but he wasn't satisfied. He wanted something more, or perhaps someone else. The meekness that he used to find so endearing now bothered him immensely. She was almost too obedient. He liked being in control, but he enjoyed it more when he had to fight for it, like in the courtroom. He also missed the body she had when she was dancing. He vividly remembered being able to lift her up onto the kitchen counter or table and, when the kids weren't home, doing unspeakable things in the kitchen. Now, sex was more of a craving that he fulfilled with her and less about sharing a mutual attraction. Yet, despite all this, he knew that he should call her on their anniversary, if not to pretend, then at least to avoid the comments Nancy loved to half mutter under her breath.

"Happy anniversary!" he exclaimed, feigning excitement. "Thanks for the text!"

"Oh you're welcome!" she responded. "I was just thinking of you. Do you wanna go out to dinner tonight instead of cooking together? Ariana and Teddy are here."

"I'm sorry, but I have to work late. I have to be in court at 10 tomorrow and I haven't gotten a chance to really sit with the file today. It's been crazy here. Maybe we can go out this weekend," he said.

"Okay," she said.

Damn it, fight me, he thought.

"In that case, I'm going to bed early. Have a good night." Nancy hung up, and her face dropped. She was sick of him working late and didn't care if he had a legitimate excuse for tonight or not. He had slipped into bed late at night most of last week smelling like whiskey and scotch. She wondered if he was doing more than drinking at the bars but tried not to think too much about it.

Nancy stared at her cell phone and sighed. Ariana, who was doing homework at the kitchen table, looked up to see her mother's dismal expression.

"What's wrong, Mom?" she asked, putting her pencil down.

"Oh, nothing," Nancy replied, sauntering into the kitchen. She opened the fridge and was greeted by the food that was supposed to be her anniversary dinner. She didn't want it to go to waste, but she wasn't sure she had the motivation to cook it anymore. She shut the door.

"Were you and Dad supposed to have a special dinner tonight or something?" she asked.

"Yeah. It's our anniversary," Nancy said, trying not to show any more emotion than she already had.

"Well, where is Dad then? Shouldn't you guys be celebrating?" Nancy tried to keep herself composed, but felt as though her daughter had stabbed her in the chest and took a deep breath to overcome the pain.

"He has to work late," she said. *Is there really anything to celebrate?* she thought to herself. She suddenly wondered if maybe it was a good thing he had cancelled on her. At least now they wouldn't have to sit at opposite ends of the table and pretend they were still in love, the two-sided facade they'd both been keeping up for years.

"Dad's not coming home?" Teddy yelled over the

noise of the video game he was playing.

"No," Nancy confirmed.

"Well, why don't we all cook together?" Ariana suggested, looking for any excuse to get away from the pile of homework she had to do.

"I suppose we could," Nancy said. "Teddy, do you like salmon?" she yelled into the other room.

"Eh, it's alright," he yelled back over the cascade of gunfire coming from his video game.

Ariana removed herself from her homework and went into the kitchen to join her mother. Ariana opened the fridge and was amazed by the amount of food. Their fridge was usually pretty sparse, but today it was overflowing with peppers, squash, onions, spinach, lemons, tilapia and salmon.

"What about tilapia?" Ariana yelled to Teddy as she approached the living room.

"That's better," he yelled back.

"Then come help us make it," Ariana said, planting herself in front of his game and crossing her arms over her chest.

"Move, you're gonna get me killed!"

"That's kind of the point," she said, rolling her eyes.

The game made a whirring noise and a notice that Teddy's character had been killed flashed on the screen.

"When did you get so bitchy?" he said bitterly.

"Since Dad designated me as the golden child," she said coolly.

"Well excuse me, little Miss Perfect," Teddy said, throwing his joystick on the ground, getting up from his bean bag chair, and pushing past her into the kitchen.

"Hey, stop fighting!" Nancy yelled from the kitchen. "This is supposed to be family night."

Ariana turned around and followed Teddy into the kitchen. *Actually, it's supposed to be your anniversary dinner*, Ariana thought, refraining herself from saying it out loud.

"Dad's working late again?" Teddy half-asked as he leaned up against the counter in the center of the kitchen.

"Yes," Nancy sighed.

"He must be drowning then," Teddy said, "I haven't had to hide out at Dexter's nearly as much lately."

"Yeah, I guess he is," Nancy said. *Maybe drowning in alcohol*, she thought to herself.

"Yeah, it's been nice," Ariana said. "He hasn't been harassing me about school lately, which is good because I'm dying in math right now."

Nancy grabbed a couple peppers out of the fridge and started washing them. She then placed them on a cutting board she had already laid out on the center counter and started chopping.

"What can we do to help?" Ariana asked.

"Why doesn't one of you filet the fish and the other make a sauce for it?"

"I call the sauce!" Ariana interjected before Teddy could react. He was still a little high from earlier in the day but it was gradually fading off. He grudgingly went to the fridge and pulled out the fish. He rummaged through a cabinet next to the fridge in search of another cutting board while Ariana looked in their spice cabinet on the other end of kitchen for seasonings. Once everyone had assembled their ingredients and began preparing them, a silence fell over the room. Teddy noticed it first, but decided to wait for someone else to break it. He didn't want to be the one to point out that three people who lived together had nothing to talk about.

Nancy broke the silence by asking Ariana about her party on Friday. She informed her that she might be getting dinner with one of her friends that night and that Ariana would need to find a ride to and from the party.

"Dan should be able to pick me up and drop me off," Ariana said. "I may actually be able to sleep over Kelsey's too."

"Wait, Dan's going to this party too? I thought this was a small, girls only thing?"

"It's small," Ariana said quickly, "but it's more of a couples party," she lied.

"So Kelsey's parents are okay with a bunch of high schoolers 'sleeping' on their floor?"

"They trust us," Ariana said, trying to reassure her mother. "And not everyone is sleeping over, they just wanted us to know it's an option if we really have to.

"'Really have to?' Is there going to be alcohol?"

Ariana fell silent for a moment, trying to figure out how to best approach the situation. Nancy took her silence as a "yes" and promptly said, "You're not going to this party. I bet if I called her parents this second, they wouldn't have a clue as to what their daughter has planned."

"But Mom!" Ariana protested, dropping the spoon she was stirring the sauce with against the side of the glass bowl.

"No buts, when I get home from dinner with Barb on Friday, you better be in bed. You said you would do Zumba with me and there's a class at 10 a.m. on Saturday," Nancy said, chopping methodically.

"Ugh, this is so unfair! I don't have to drink! I can go to a party and go to Zumba the next morning."

"In case you haven't noticed, addiction runs in this family," Nancy said, glancing sideways at Teddy, "The only way to combat it is to avoid temptation."

"Have you ever noticed that all we do in this family is fight?" Teddy said, dropping the knife he was filleting the fish with.

"Are we airing our grievances now?" Ariana said. "Because I'd love to tell you how much everyone hates your slacker attitude! You've been unemployed for two months, Teddy! And you haven't even been looking for a new job because you've been too busy getting high and playing video games."

Teddy's mouth fell open. "Since when did you become an insufferable bitch?" he retorted. "You think you're better than everyone else just because you're taking honors classes and are dating the star pitcher of the baseball team."

Ariana's face got red and she was about to respond when Nancy interjected.

"Okay, that's enough."

"No, you know what, this is good," Ariana said. "Tell me how you really feel, Teddy."

"Okay, well you know what," Teddy said, "Dad was still a lot harder on me than he is on you just because you're a girl. You can't even begin to understand."

"Sorry I was born with boobs!" she replied. "And at least Dad cared about your soccer career. He doesn't give a shit about dance and I actually have potential to go somewhere with it!"

"God, you're conceited. What, do you think you're a music video sensation or something?"

"I could be," she said seriously. Teddy rolled his eyes in response. "You wouldn't know though. I think you came to one of my recitals and that was ten years ago."

Nancy stood with her mouth agape with horror at the way her children were treating each other. She had seen them fight as kids, but didn't remember them being so cruel. She didn't know whether to scream or cry, so she said nothing as Ariana stormed away and Teddy slammed a pan onto the stovetop.

"What's wrong with her?" Teddy asked his mom.

"What's wrong with all of us?" she asked rhetorically. Silence fell over the kitchen as she and Teddy continued to prepare dinner.

Upstairs, Ariana had locked herself in her room and was crying into her pillow. *Am I conceited?* she wondered. She couldn't help but think that her father was also arrogant. She wondered if she was becoming him and, if she was, if there was a way to stop it. A little voice in the back of her head told her to apologize, but she was still too angry at Teddy to walk back downstairs. When she was sure her tear ducts were dry, she scrolled through Facebook for twenty minutes to numb her mind and went back downstairs, her face still a little puffy.

"I'm sorry," Ariana said as she entered the kitchen. "I think I've just been so stressed with school and I took it out on you."

"It's alright," Teddy said. "You're right, I should start looking for a job." They hugged, and Ariana helped her mother and brother finish making dinner.

"I wish you two still got along like you did when you were younger," Nancy said, flipping the fish over in the pan. They spent the rest of dinner reminiscing about how great things seemed to be when they were younger, each one of them silently wondering how they could recapture those moments in the present.

* * *

Frank had made quick work of the file he was finishing up after he got off the phone with Nancy and decided to call his friend Andy.

"Hey, do you wanna hit CJ's tonight?" Frank asked. He quickly organized the papers on his desk as he worked the details out with Andy on speaker phone.

The two men met in the parking lot of their hometown bar, C. J. Sparrows, and walked in together. Frank wasted no time once he sat down.

"I'll take a Scotch on the rocks please," he said to the bartender, who was in the middle of making someone else's drink.

"Hold on a sec," the bartender said with an annoyed look on his face.

"Fine, fine," Frank muttered to himself.

"What's wrong man?" Andy asked as he shrugged his coat off onto the bar stool behind him.

"Nothing," Frank said, tapping his fingers on the

bar.

"Really? Because you haven't called me in over a month."

"I've been busy, okay?" Frank said. Andy was only half listening and didn't notice Frank's sharp tone because he was busy ordering himself a beer. The bartender quickly opened a bottle for Andy and eyed Frank, who was still waiting on his Scotch.

"With what?" Andy asked.

"With work man. I've been busting my ass since Nancy started talking about quitting her job," he said through gritted teeth. In reality, he'd been drinking with his co-workers because he thought they were better company.

"Oh geez. Well hey, at least she can get something else lined up." The bartender served Frank his scotch with a grimace and Frank handed his card over to open up a tab. "When did she say she was leaving?"

"Um, about a week ago. I don't know if she actually gave her two weeks yet or not."

"Is she looking?" Andy asked as he turned to face Frank.

"Kind of. I think her idea of looking is browsing on Indeed and never actually applying."

"Maybe she's looking for ideas," Andy suggested, slowly sipping his beer.

"And maybe she's full of shit," Frank said, swallowing the remainder of his scotch in one gulp and promptly ordering a second. Not knowing how to respond, Andy quickly finished his beer and ordered another. He was too sober to deal with other people's problems, especially problems of this magnitude. He took a long swig the second the bartender handed him his beer. The two men sat in silence for a while, observing the people around them. On their right, a young couple was having a casual dinner of burgers and fries. They were each sipping purple drinks that reminded Frank of the grape soda he used to love as a kid. A rowdy group of 20-something guys was seated at a table beyond the couple, but the two men tried to drown them out with their thoughts. Neither wanted to think about a time when they were young, happy, and drunk, when in reality they were old, miserable, and sober.

A group of four middle aged women who were trying to relive their twenties were sitting at a table on the far left. Three were dressed in crop tops and skirts that were too short for them and were falling all over themselves. The other was wearing a tight black A-line skirt and a loose white blouse and appeared to be fairly sober. Frank found his gaze lingering on the blond woman in her business casual clothing and slowly turned to face his drink. He wondered if she had just come from an important meeting, or if she was the designated driver and, as such, felt the need to dress like a chauffeur. He ordered a third scotch before he nudged Andy and motioned in her direction.

"What's up with that get-up?" Frank asked.

"I don't know man, you tell me," Andy responded, "you're the one wearing a suit to the bar at eight pm."

"I couldn't go home to change. Nancy thinks I'm working late."

"Oh, so there's a lot of trouble in paradise," Andy said with a slight smile. "Who knows, maybe she hasn't changed for the same reason," he said, motioning to the blonde with the same hand that held his beer.

"Is it bad that I want to find out what it is?"

"It's bad if you don't," Andy grinned. Frank returned his smile. He was glad he had called Andy, a man who had been successfully cheating on his wife for the past five years and thinking nothing of it.

"We only had sex once," he had said to Frank, even though they both knew he was lying. Frank hadn't been sure what to think, but didn't want to think too hard about the situation, especially now. He couldn't exactly understand why this woman was attractive to him, as one of her brunette friends was showing off quite the figure for someone her age. Had she not been with women who looked older than her, she probably could have passed for thirty.

"So?" Andy said, interrupting Frank's reverie about sleeping with the blonde. "Are you gonna talk to her or not?"

"Yeah," Frank said. "Wait, do you think this is a good idea? What if Nancy finds out?"

"How's she gonna find out?" Andy flashed him an evil smile. Frank smiled back nervously and ordered a beer. The two men sat in silence, glancing back at the group of women every so often. Frank was busy trying to calm his nerves and Andy was busy trying to decide if he should add a second mistress to the mix. When Frank was done giving himself a silent pep talk, he turned to Andy.

"Will you go over there with me?" Frank asked.

"Sure," Andy said, lowering his voice, "that leopard print screams desperate." The two men grabbed their beers and approached the group of girls. They began talking to the two they weren't interested in first (a trick they had perfected in college) and the blonde and the woman in the leopard print soon joined in the conversation out of curious jealousy. Frank smiled at the blonde and looked away, feigning shyness. She asked him his name and she told him that her name was Isabelle. He learned that she was an executive at a consulting firm when she began complaining about work.

"As a lawyer, you must be amazed by just how incompetent some people are. I see it every day and it drives me nuts."

"Yeah," he said, "I see it all the time with our

personal injury claims. I think that's more people who don't want to work, but I still think that's incompetence."

She put her drink down on the table excitedly. "No, it definitely is! I think the problem is that people are lazy. My last secretary might have been good at her job if she had bothered to just answer the damn phones. Now we have to look for someone else. Normally that'd be HR's job, but at my company, they want the executives involved in all hiring decisions. So I have to sit in on all the interviews."

"Yeah, I'm glad I don't have to worry about hiring anybody."

Their conversation took on a life of its own while Andy continued entertaining the other three women with his tales of drunken debauchery. He winked at Frank and Frank suggested that he and Isabelle move to a more private table. Isabelle agreed and they moved to a table near the door of the restaurant. They continued talking about how much they hated people and Frank bit his tongue every time he thought of Nancy. Then, discovering that keeping her out of conversation would be nearly impossible, he created a new persona for her: Andy's wife.

"Yeah, my friend over there," he said, pointing to Andy, "his wife is so bad sometimes. She gets pissed at him for going to the bar, but never says so. She just acts super pissed off at him the next morning and doesn't want him to have any fun without her."

Isabelle sipped the cosmopolitan that Frank had bought her and set it down. "Well does he go to the bars a lot? Because I would be mad if my husband cared more about drinking than about me."

Frank sat back in his chair, began to consider what she said, and then decided that all women were the same and that there was nothing wrong with going to happy hour every night.

"Well, I'm a free spirit," he said, "so I wouldn't care."

Isabelle sipped her drink slowly then set it down on the ring of condensation it had already created on the table. "I mean, I'm a free spirit too, but that's why I'm single."

"Ah, then we have something in common," Frank said, smiling with his eyes.

"You mean being single?" she asked with a sultry bat of her eyes.

Frank nodded. "All of the above," he said. She gave him a longing glance and Frank felt his heart jump a bit.

"Well, what are two attractive single people to do when they find each other at a bar at night?" she asked, smiling seductively. She slowly began to slide her leg up his.

"I can think of a lot of things," Frank said, returning her smile. He shifted in his seat to readjust himself.

"Why don't you close out your tab then?" she said, her leg continuing its journey up to Frank's thigh.

"Wow, you cut right to the chase, don't you?"

"I believe in efficiency," she said. "Why waste time chasing when we can both get what we want right now?"

"I guess there's no better time than the present," Frank said. He stood up and walked over to the bar to close his tab. They left within the next ten minutes and went straight to Isabelle's house.

Nancy was asleep when Frank came home at two in the morning smelling like scotch and cigarettes. He silently cursed the fact that Isabelle smoked as he took off his smoke-scented clothes in his car and left them there, praying that none of his neighbors would see him sneaking into his own house in boxers. As he carefully climbed into bed next to Nancy, he made a mental note to remember that he had clothes in his car and to wash them himself the next day. Frank thought he heard Nancy mumble something and froze. Even though he was safely in bed with his wife and he and Isabelle had agreed to a one-time fling, he was wary. He didn't understand how Andy could be so nonchalant about cheating.

6

The Broken Heart

Nancy mentally braced herself as she sat in her car in the parking lot. She had just left her second job interview in years and was still replaying the whole thing over in her head, not to mention worrying about what would happen in a few short minutes. She took two deep breaths before she stepped out of the car and walked into the cardiologist's office.

She wasn't expecting Dr. Melnyk, the cardiologist her doctor had referred her to, to say much more than "lose some weight" — which she had already resolved to do — so when the cardiologist took the time to sit down in a chair to talk to her after her EKG, she knew something was wrong.

"Your EKG confirmed that you're presenting with symptoms of heart disease," Dr. Melnyk said, her bespectacled face looking disapprovingly at Nancy as she glanced up from the clipboard she had on her lap. "We're going to run some more tests, but I want to put you on an ACE inhibitor as a preventative measure and see how you do. You should also exercise and work on eating healthy. You're extremely lucky that you haven't had a heart attack yet."

Nancy sat there in stunned shock. "What if the medication doesn't work?"

"Then you may need to have surgery," Dr. Melnyk said, looking Nancy directly in the eyes. "Don't worry though, most patients can manage the condition and never need surgery. I do want you to get blood work done though." Dr. Melnyk tore a prescription off her clipboard and handed it to Nancy.

Tears welled up in Nancy's eyes. She couldn't imagine needing heart surgery at fifty-one. She didn't want to think about the cost or the disapproving look in her husband's eyes. The cost of the medication itself was a burden she didn't want her husband to know about. She thanked the doctor and went back out into her car to cry.

After about ten minutes of hysteria, she finally managed to pull herself together, although she couldn't shake the shame that plagued her mind as she started driving. *How did this happen? How did I let myself go like this?* She remembered how hard she had worked as a dancer, how she would wake up early to not only condition, but to focus on her technique and form. She used to spend countless hours in front of a mirror for the sake of improvement and now she tried to avoid mirrors at all cost. This realization made her cry more, but also reminded her that she could recapture this same mindset if she tried. Her tears began to dry now that she knew a solution was in sight and at that exact moment, she caught sight of a gym about 100 feet away on her right. She stopped short and veered into the parking lot. She parked and tried to take a few deep breaths, but they came out strained and made her cough a little. *Geez, do I have congestive heart failure too?* she wondered. She turned her car off and tried to slow her racing mind before she went inside. *What if they judge me? What if I can't afford it? I know I have another interview tomorrow, but what if I can't find a job? Oh, why did I have to give my two weeks' notice the other day? How did I let this happen?*

Finally, she convinced herself to get out of the car and walk towards the gym. When she walked through the door, a toned, tan young man greeted her behind the counter. She was glad that his smile seemed genuine and not judgmental.

"Hi, how can I help you?" he asked.

"Well, I want to start working out again," Nancy said, "and I don't really know where to begin."

The man instantly perked up and picked up an ad that was lying on the counter Nancy was approaching.

"You picked a good time to start," he said, holding up the ad for Nancy to see.

"We have a personal training promo going on right now. You can get two weeks' worth of personal training for just $25 a session. It's kind of like a trial period before you decide to commit to a regimen. Most people do three to four sessions a week."

Nancy did the mental math and nodded. One hundred and fifty dollars to jump start a routine didn't sound too awful. "Wow, that sounds perfect. What's the catch?"

The man sighed. "After the two weeks is up, the rate increases to $55 per session."

Nancy's eyes bugged out of her head and the man motioned for her to lean in close. "I don't know what these owners are thinking with this 'deal' though. I would personally just take the discounted weeks to learn some moves and then work out on my own afterwards." He leaned back again and said louder, "Our most basic membership is only $10 a month."

Glad that there was a loophole, Nancy smiled and said she would sign up for the two-week personal training promotion. She grudgingly pulled out her credit card and paid, hoping Frank wasn't monitoring her statements again. She walked out to her car with more confidence than she had walked in with. She decided to ride the high of her confidence all the way to the grocery store, where she stocked up on healthier foods.

Nancy arrived home with three bags of groceries and laid them on the counter before she ran to the bathroom. When she came out, she saw that Ariana had started unpacking the bags. Ariana's face screwed up when she picked up a packet of marinated beets. She held them far away from her, as if they were diseased.

"Mom, since when do you eat beets?"

"Since I'm trying to lose weight," Nancy replied, taking a heavy step forward as if to prove her point.

A wave of understanding washed over Ariana. She had suspected that was the case since her mother had expressed interest in Zumba and boxing but hadn't wanted to offend her.

"Well that's great, Mom!" Ariana walked around the counter and embraced Nancy. "I'm so proud of you!"

Nancy smiled and wiped a tear from her face before pulling away. "Thanks! That's why there's all that spinach and kale in there too. Those are supposed to be extra good for you."

Ariana readjusted her ponytail, which had gotten pulled a bit in the hug, before replying. She had a mixture of joy and confusion on her face that was hard for Nancy to place.

"So what made you decide to eat healthy and do

Zumba and everything?" Ariana said. "I mean, it's great and all, you've just never said anything about it before."

Nancy hesitated a moment. Her eyes darted down to the ground before meeting Ariana's again. "Well, I was watching you dance the other day and it reminded me of how thin and graceful I used to feel. Even though I can't dance anymore, I'd still like to recapture that feeling." Nancy paused, giving a moment of silence to her glory days. "And we all know I'm not getting any younger."

Sadness washed over Ariana's face and she went to hug her mother again.

"I'm so sorry, Mom. I never really thought about how hard it might be for you to watch me dance before."

"No, no honey, I'm so proud of you. I only wish I could join you."

"Maybe you can. Not like you used to because you might re-injure yourself, but you can start with Zumba, like you were talking about before."

Nancy paused for a moment and smiled. "Yeah, remember, you said you'd go with me on Saturday morning."

"Right!" Ariana said. She suddenly remembered that this Saturday was the first Saturday in a month that she didn't have her own dance class at 9am and swore quietly at herself for signing up for Zumba on her one day off from dance. She went up to her room, plopped down on her bed and started texting Dan.

Hey, how's it going? she texted.

Alright, just struggling through Bally's homework right now, he responded.

Ah, I should be doing that, she replied. *I should ask Marcy for help*, she said.

Yeah, she's helping me right now, he responded.

Ariana dropped her phone and began wondering why on earth he had gone to Marcy for help without asking her if she had even started the homework yet. She wasn't expecting Dan to ask her for help, but at least to want to struggle through their math homework together. This was the third time Dan had gone to Marcy for help without even considering her and she had already told him the second time they had this fight that they should just form a study group.

Wish I was invited, she replied, unafraid of her bitterness. She hadn't imagined she'd ever come so close to telling him what was really on her mind for fear of scaring him off, but she was beyond the point of caring. They had been dating for almost a year and she was wondering if they'd be dating for much longer.

Sorry, Dan said. Ariana stared at her screen waiting for a follow up text saying that he had completely spaced out and that they should all get together later that week to study for the upcoming test, but it never came. Aggravated, Ariana put her phone on her bedside table and lay in her bed, staring up at the ceiling.

What if they're doing more than just studying? she wondered. She imagined them huddled over Dan's textbook, Marcy's silky auburn hair creating a thin curtain between their faces. She imagined him pushing Marcy's hair aside and leaning in for a kiss. She found herself involuntarily shaking her head no and snapped out of her waking nightmare. She was glad she hadn't had sex with him yet.

She was holding off mostly because there was a part of her that was scared of the unknown of sex, but also because there was a part of her that was scared of losing her virginity to the wrong person. The more she and Dan seemed to drift apart, the more and more she wondered if he was the right person. He had been so different when they first started dating that she wondered if he was even the same person he used to be.

7

The Interview Aftermath

Frank came home late the next night, but this time Nancy was sitting at the kitchen table, drinking tea. She looked anxious, and Frank's heart skipped a beat.

"What are you doing up this late?" he asked, setting his keys down on the counter.

"Waiting for you," she replied, fingering the string attached to her teabag. Her eyes glanced down at her mug and then met his. He knew she was bracing herself for an argument and felt his body stiffen in response.

"What's up?" he asked.

"I got a job today," she said. Her lips were smiling but her eyes betrayed her anger. She had smelled the smoke on his skin when he had crawled into bed on Monday night and suspected he hadn't picked up the habit overnight.

"That's great honey!" Frank's face lit up and he

went to embrace her. She didn't reciprocate his half hug over the back of her chair. He felt the memory of his affair slipping into his mind. *Does she know I was complaining about her? Does she know I slept with someone else?* he thought.

"I was planning on telling you when I got the call earlier today," she said, standing up and turning around to face Frank, "but I haven't seen you in almost forty-eight hours."

"I've been working late," Frank said, looking away from her penetrating eyes.

"Really?" she said, turning around to walk into the kitchen. She placed her tea mug in the sink and turned around, "you must have had a lot of scotch at the office then because I could smell you breathing it in my face last night."

"Oh, well I went out after I finished work," he said. Nancy looked at him disapprovingly and he swallowed hard. "But it was only because I finished so late. It was around nine when I finally wrapped up and I just needed a drink. You were already in bed and I was too stressed to go right to sleep."

"I stay up late sometimes," she said, leaning up against the counter. Some sadistic part of her enjoyed watching him squirm and she tried to conceal a smile.

"You expect me to know when you decide to? Half the time when I call home you tell me not to bother coming home."

"The fact that you even ask if I want you to come home after work is absurd! Isn't that part of the unwritten contract we signed when we got married? Of course when you call and ask, 'Will I be missing anything exciting later?' I'm not going to lie and say there is when your family should be exciting enough." Nancy felt her face get hot and a searing pain ripped across her chest. She almost doubled over but leaned over the counter for support. She didn't want to show any weakness, especially not when she was winning an argument. Thankfully, Frank was too stunned to speak for a moment and the wave of pain receded as quickly as it came on. Frank was so busy racing through his thoughts for a come-back that he didn't even notice that his wife had a fit of pain in the middle of their argument.

"I know you don't want to come home," Nancy said vindictively, channeling the adrenaline from the pain into anger, "so why should I make you do something you don't want to do?"

Frank didn't have a response, but stood stiffly as he felt blood rush to his face. He was angry at Nancy for starting the fight and angrier at himself for not knowing how to finish it. Nancy stormed past him to go upstairs. She tore into their bedroom and the cat, who was curled up on her bed, flew off and scurried into the closet. Nancy followed the cat into the closet, grabbed a blanket, and walked back out into her bedroom in a huff. She grabbed Frank's pillows and threw them downstairs along with the blanket.

"Sleep on the couch tonight!" she yelled. She stormed off into her room and locked her door.

Ariana, who had heard the whole argument, didn't know what to think. She had never heard her parents argue like that before. She had heard her dad yell plenty of times, but her mom usually didn't raise her voice, nor had she ever kicked her father out of their room before. After Ariana heard her mother's door close and lock, she poked her head out of her room and darted across the hall to Teddy's room. She knocked lightly on his door and whispered a greeting, but was met with silence. She turned around and went back to her room to fall asleep.

8

Secrets, Secrets Are No Fun

The next morning, Frank found himself gripping the steering wheel tightly, his hands sweating even though it was only 50 degrees. Nancy sat calmly in the passenger's seat, her brown leather purse on her lap. She was wearing a button-down green blouse and brown dress pants. With her heavy-set figure, she reminded Frank of an overgrown bush. He looked down at his own slim figure and tried to remember the last time he had eaten. He had been so stressed about work and Nancy finding out about Isabelle that food hadn't been his top priority the past few days.

When Nancy's car had refused to start that morning, Frank had taken it as a sign that his wife wasn't meant to work, especially not at this new job. Nancy, however, had taken it as an obstacle to be overcome and insisted that Frank drive her to work.

"It's only half an hour away," she had said. She

wasn't exactly thrilled about driving in with him either but knew that her destination was just far enough away to make Uber a complete waste of money.

"Where is it again?" he asked, sipping his coffee in the driver's seat. He had a busy day at work and didn't want his wife's problems to derail his progress.

"New Haven. It's a consulting firm."

A flash of panic washed over Frank's face. He felt his stomach jump to his throat but swallowed hard and tried to convince himself that it was just a coincidence. *Hadn't Isabelle mentioned that she worked in New Haven and was hiring a new receptionist?* He wondered how Andy did it. The paranoia was beginning to fully set in.

"Ugh, it's gonna take me forever to get in and out of there."

"Come on, Frank," Nancy spat, "I promise this is the last favor I'll ever ask."

Frank plugged the address into his GPS and put the car into drive, complaining about how he had so much work to do and how much of an inconvenience driving her to work was. Nancy tried to ignore him, but by the time they reached the parking lot, she found herself irritated enough to punch him in the face. He found a parking spot away from everybody else and stopped the car.

"You ready?" he asked Nancy.

"Yep," she said, unbuckling her seat belt. Right as she got out, he noticed a car pull in two spots over from him. He saw Isabelle get out of the car and wave to Nancy, but Nancy didn't see her. His heart jumped to his throat and his hand moved to start the car when Nancy opened the door and said, "Hold on a minute," before shutting it. Frank tried to contain himself as she rustled through her purse for something. He saw Isabelle approaching his wife from behind and panicked.

He rolled down the window and said, "Hey honey, I really got to get to work," right as Isabelle tapped on Nancy's shoulder in passing. Nancy said hi to her and started engaging in small talk. She suddenly remembered that her husband was waiting in the car.

"Isabelle, I'd like you to meet my husband, Frank."

"Hi," Frank said meekly through the open window.

Isabelle caught his eye and gave him a stunned look. He remembered that he had told Isabelle he was single and saw her smile slip into a sneer. "Nice to meet you," Isabelle said. Frank quickly pulled away as the two women walked towards the office.

* * *

Nancy was eating her lunch in the cafeteria when

Isabelle smiled at her and sat down next to her.

"How do you like it so far?" Isabelle asked, sticking a fork in her salad.

"Good!" Nancy said, putting her sandwich down and wiping her mouth, "It's a lot more streamlined than the office I used to work in. I feel like there's a system for everything here, so I really just need to learn the process."

"That's awesome! You're already so much better than the last girl we had." Isabelle lowered her eyes and took a bite of her salad.

"Well you've been pretty good at checking in on me too and keeping me on task. Thank you so much for everything."

"Don't thank me just yet," Isabelle muttered under her breath.

"Excuse me?" Nancy said, a lump forming in her throat, "Am I doing something wrong?"

"No, you're doing great. It's just," Isabelle trailed off and lowered her eyes.

"What?" Nancy said.

"By some strange coincidence, I slept with your husband the other night. I didn't know he was married. He told me he was single and I believed him. I'm so sorry, I never would have done it if I knew he was married to anyone."

Nancy sat there, speechless. Her suspicions about her husband had been confirmed, but beyond reassuring her that she hadn't been making up stories in her head, this knowledge didn't make her feel any better.

"Nancy, are you okay? I'm sorry, I know this must be hard to hear but I just know that I couldn't look you in the eye every day if I kept it from you."

"It's fine," Nancy said, "I'm sure you weren't the first."

Nancy looked back down at the sandwich she had been hungry enough to finish five minutes ago. Now the smell of tuna nauseated her and she put her sandwich back in its Ziploc bag and zipped everything into her lunchbox.

"If you'll excuse me, I think I need to be alone right now," she said, standing up. Isabelle nodded and Nancy proceeded to the bathroom, where she splashed cold water on her face in an effort to hide the tears that were beginning to form in the corners of her eyes. *How did I get here?* she asked herself, staring down her reflection in the mirror.

* * *

Later that night, Ariana found herself home alone. Her mother had gone out with a long-lost friend that Ariana hadn't known existed until this past week, and her father had told her mother that he'd be working late. Teddy was never home anyway, and Ariana assumed he was either at Dexter's or smoking alone in his car.

She was in her bedroom, reading a magazine and checking the clock every so often until Dan called her.

"You almost ready?" he asked.

"I thought the party wasn't until 9:30?" she said, pulling her phone away from her ear to double check the time.

"It is, but Bryce asked me to bring some booze and my brother is out of town. Can Teddy grab us some?"

"Phhh," she said, "I don't even know where he is."

"Shit! I can't show up empty handed. Wait, your dad has a lot of booze, right?"

"Dan, I'm not going to get murdered because you made a promise you couldn't keep. We're not stealing my Dad's booze. He drinks it all the time, he's gonna notice."

"Okay, fine," Dan said, "I'll figure something else out."

"Okay, I'll see you at 8:30," she said, rolling her eyes. *Why on earth does he think it's okay to ask me to steal from my dad?*

They said goodbye and she hung up the phone. Before he had asked her to steal her father's alcohol, she had contemplated texting him in fifteen minutes and saying that her parents weren't home and that he could come over earlier, but now she was glad she hadn't. She wanted to just make out and cuddle and she knew he would take her parents being gone as an invitation to have sex. Now she no longer wanted to even kiss him.

She found herself thinking about how much he wanted to have sex though. While he had never explicitly pressured her, he sometimes sighed heavily whenever he asked if she wanted to and she said no. She sometimes felt guilty, but she tried not to think about it too much. *He needs to respect my decision*, she thought to herself. She stood up and walked towards her mirror, examining her face. Light brown freckles danced below her green eyes and her long black hair framed her face, making it look more angular than it really was. She pushed her hair behind her ears and leaned in closer to the mirror, checking for acne. She had a small zit on her chin, but her skin was flawless otherwise. She leaned back from the mirror and walked into the bathroom that she and Teddy shared.

She was hit with the smell of Axe and weed the second she opened the door and she coughed a little. She bent down and opened the third and last drawer on the right. She pulled out her curling iron and plugged it in to heat it up. She then reached into the top right drawer and pulled out her make up bag. She applied a thin layer of foundation and then spot-treated her zit. She suddenly remembered she should be dressed before she curled her hair, so she ran into her room and pulled her Halloween costume out of her closet. She threw the robe on her bed and fished her boxing gloves off of the floor of her closet. She yanked open the drawer that hosted both her sports bra and spandex and changed. She then hurried back into the bathroom to discover that her curling iron was warmed up. Satisfied with her outfit, she started curling her hair, unable to stop smiling. She realized how much her life had changed since Dan had become the starting varsity pitcher towards the end of last season. She had gone from being a quiet loner last year to a girl who was now dating one of the most popular boys in school. It didn't matter to her that he wasn't popular when they had started dating; it just mattered that now they were able to ascend the ranks of their school's hierarchy together.

Her phone, which was sitting on the bathroom vanity, lit up with a notification. She tapped it with her free hand to see that Kelsey was texting her.

You're picking me and David up tonight, right?

Ariana finished curling a section of her hair and put her curling iron down to respond.

Yeah, getting ready now.

She grabbed another section of hair and wound it around the curling iron.

Okay, what time are you getting us?

Ariana finished the section of hair she was working on and put the curling iron down again to respond.

I think around 9:15.

She picked her curling iron up again and finished curling her hair without checking her phone anymore. She walked into her room and turned her clock radio on for background noise. She scanned to find her favorite late-night talk show. One of the callers had just asked when one should have sex with a new partner and Ariana found herself listening intently. She walked into the bathroom, grabbed her make up bag, and brought it into her room to put on some finishing touches to her eye make-up. The women who were calling into the show to voice their opinions all seemed to have different ideas as to when it was appropriate to have sex, from the first date to six months into the relationship. Ariana breathed a sigh of relief that there was no "normal" and that it was okay to want to wait, especially for her first time. She finished doing her make-up and sat down on her bed, still listening to the radio.

She heard a horn and realized that it was getting late. She looked at the clock, saw that it was 8:15, and checked her phone. Dan had texted her five minutes ago that he was at her house. She quickly grabbed a red purse from her closet, dropped her phone in it, and threw it on her bed. She then shrugged on her robe, picked up her purse and boxing gloves, and ran down the stairs and out the front door, quickly locking it behind her.

"Why are you so early?" she asked as she got into his car.

"Because we need to figure out how to get booze," he said, starting the car and putting it in gear.

"Why can't Bryce provide the booze? It's his party."

"Because he doesn't have any hook ups."

"And you do?"

"Well, I have my brother and your brother," he responded, glaring at her.

"I don't even count on my brother so I don't know why on earth you do," she said.

Dan didn't respond and started driving. Abut ten minutes into the drive, Ariana lost track of where they were and each subsequent street began looking darker and more daunting.

"Where are we going?" Ariana said.

"I think Scott has a fake," he responded, turning onto another unfamiliar road. A guy dressed in all black pushed a bike in front of him down the car lined street. Trash littered the street, and couches and commodes sat on front lawns with large "For Sale" signs taped to them.

"Where are we?" she asked, "Deliverance?"

Dan scoffed and pulled into a driveway. "Well it's not your perfect little town of Cheshire, but it's not that bad." He pulled out his phone and sent a quick text. Ariana looked around uneasily. She manually locked her door and tried to relax. Right as she was beginning to melt back into her seat, Scott opened the door to the back seat and got in, kicking the back of her seat in the process. She bolted upright. The party hadn't even started yet and it didn't seem like it was going to be a good night. She considered feigning sickness as Scott and Dan exchanged pleasantries and Dan asked him how to get to the nearest liquor store. Ariana was still silently contemplating the idea of retching as Dan started driving and he and Scott started talking about drinking and baseball. The car slowly meandered out of residential areas and onto the main road. Dan pulled into a small liquor store on the main strip and told Scott to grab him a thirty rack and a handle of vodka. He handed him $40 and they watched Scott get out of the car. Dan watched him go into the store and leaned in to kiss Ariana as the door shut behind Scott. Ariana kissed back and within two minutes they were making out.

"I really wanna do it tonight," he said, pulling away and looking into her eyes.

"I don't know if I'm ready," she whispered.

"It's not as big of a deal as people make it out to be," he said, pushing her hair back behind her ear.

"I don't know," she said hesitantly.

Dan shook his head and turned around in his

seat to face the steering wheel. Ariana sat back in her seat, feeling like she had been punched in the stomach. Scott walked out right as awkward silence was beginning to permeate the car. He put the beer and vodka on the floor next to him and shut the door behind him.

"You owe me $5," he said to Dan.

"Okay," Dan said, starting the car and putting it into gear. "You can take two for yourself after we open the 30 rack then."

"Can you plug in Kelsey's address?" he asked Ariana, who had already started typing the address into her phone.

* * *

The five teenagers slipped out of the car around 9:45. There were only seven other cars there, but the well-lit house revealed a sea of teenagers inside. Ariana did the mental math and figured that there were at least thirty-five more people inside, plus whoever's parents had dropped them off at Bryce's before anyone else had shown up.

They walked into a cloud of smoke and Ariana coughed. It seemed that wherever she went, she couldn't escape the smell of weed. As her eyes adjusted to the smoke, she made out the shape of

Dan's best friends, Zach, Mike, Anna, and Marcy in the kitchen. She and Dan walked towards them, Dan carrying the beer and Ariana carrying the vodka. Dan nodded "Hello" as they passed by and unloaded the alcohol on the counter. They each grabbed a beer for themselves then walked back to their circle of friends and started catching up. Dan started talking to Scott, Zach, and Mike about baseball and Ariana started talking with Marcy and Anna. As the girls were bonding over how the only thing the boys could talk about was baseball, Ariana found herself looking for Kelsey and David, who had disappeared the second they had walked through the door. She asked Marcy and Anna if they wanted to dance and they said that they might dance if they were drunk.

"Let's take shots!" Marcy suggested.

"Yeah!" Anna seconded.

Ariana gave an unenthused, "Okay," and the girls walked over towards the counter the vodka was on. Plenty of guys had taken the beer, but the vodka was still unopened.

"Where are the shot glasses?" Ariana asked.

"We don't need them," Anna said, grabbing three solo cups, "we can just eyeball it." Marcy opened the vodka and poured roughly two shots worth of vodka into each of the three solo cups.

"Cheers girls!" she said.

"Cheers!" Ariana and Anna echoed as they threw

back their shots.

Ariana had never taken a shot before and thought she was going to vomit almost immediately. The burning in her throat was the only thing that kept her from throwing up. She didn't want to follow a shot with beer though, so she grabbed someone's half full coke that was on the counter next to her and took a big swig. She tasted more alcohol, but it was a more subdued flavor, and so she used it a chaser for the next three shots that Marcy and Anna insisted on taking. Twenty minutes later, Ariana found herself stumbling towards Dan.

"Are you okay?" he asked.

"I'm fine," she said, putting her hands on his shoulders and kissing him.

"You're feeling good, huh?" Zach said, smiling at her.

"Yeah," she said, her eyes slowly traveling from Dan to Zach, then back to Dan.

"I wanna dance," she practically begged.

"No one is dancing," he said, glancing towards the living room where only two couples were grinding to fading alternative music.

"Come on," she said. "Don't be such a party pooper."

"I'll dance with you," Zach said, looking her up and down.

"Okay," Ariana said, pushing herself off of Dan.

"Wait, you need to take a shot first," she said, grabbing his arm and leading him to the counter. She poured roughly two shots of vodka into a solo cup and Zach threw it back in two sips.

"Damn, you put a lot in there," he said.

"No, you're just being a baby," she said. "That's how much Marcy and Anna were putting in."

"You think I can't hold my liquor?" he said. He grabbed the bottle of vodka and took eight big swigs straight from the bottle. "That's like eight shots right there," he said.

"Okay, not bad," Ariana said, finishing the abandoned rum and coke that she had been working on.

"Let's dance," she said, grabbing Zach's arm and dragging him into the living room.

"Screw her," Dan muttered to himself as he watched them approach the dance floor and Marcy approached him.

"What's going on?" Marcy asked, nodding in the direction of Zach and Ariana.

"I don't want to dance so picks someone else to dance with. Real classy."

"Well two can play at that game," she said. "But we might need some privacy if we're going to play dirty," she whispered. He smiled at her and gave her a quick peck on the lips.

"Let's get out of here," he said, watching Zach twirl Ariana across the living room.

She felt her mind go numb as she was dancing and let the music move her body. She felt Zach grab the small of her back to steady her and she responded by clasping her arms onto his hulking biceps. She came to, suddenly realizing how muscular he was, and laughed as he dipped her. Suddenly, his lips met hers and she didn't know how to stop it, nor did she want to. When they pulled away, his soft green eyes melted into hers and she found herself oddly attracted to him. His hands gently guided her body so that it was pressed against his and she let Zach lead her into an upstairs bedroom. They continued kissing and he locked the door behind them. He took his shirt off and when he took off hers, she didn't protest. She leaned into every kiss, every caress, and let the world slip away. It wasn't until he paused to take his pants off that she realized that she was lying naked on someone else's bed and saw Zach standing next to her.

"We shouldn't do this," she said. He got back on the bed, lowered himself down to hover over her, and kissed her.

"I know," he said breathlessly, "but that's what makes it feel so right." He kissed her neck seductively and she felt her stomach flip nervously. She couldn't tell if it was her anxiety or all the alcohol she had drank, but all she knew was that she was in a tough position.

"But Dan," she protested, suddenly remembering that she had a boyfriend.

"Shhh," he said, gently caressing her face, "he doesn't need to know." He gently kissed her neck and she felt herself melting into the bed.

She couldn't tell if it was the pure ecstasy she was in or if it was the alcohol, but she let Zach lower himself on top of her.

* * *

Ariana didn't know how late it was when she came to, but the party was winding down. She looked around and found herself in a master bedroom. Something stirred next to her and she jumped. She looked down to see Zach asleep.

"No," she whispered to herself. "No, no no," she muttered. The second she stood up, her stomach lurched, and she ran into the master bathroom to vomit. After about ten minutes of retching, she returned to the bedroom and put on her sports bra and spandex. She stumbled downstairs to find Bryce and a few of his close friends talking on the couch in his living room.

"Hey," Ariana said. She rubbed her head, which swam with alcohol with each step she took.

They glanced up at her as if she was a homeless

lady that had stumbled into their party.

"Do you know if Dan is still here?"

"No, I think he left with Marcy pretty early on," Bryce said. "He said she wasn't feeling well."

"Listen, I was," Ariana hiccuped, "Okay, am, really drunk and I don't really know what's happening. Can any of you guys drive me home on your way out?"

"We're all staying over, man," a guy wearing a backwards baseball cap said. Ariana saw the joint in his hand and knew that they weren't going to help her if they were high. She shuddered to think that if they were sober they might still refuse to drive her home.

"Fine," she said. She didn't know if it was some subconscious childhood instinct or her drunkenness, but she found herself pulling out her cell phone and dialing Teddy's number. Much to her surprise, he picked up and agreed to pick her up. Ariana made her way back up the stairs to the master bedroom to collect her things. She found her purse on the floor next to a bureau and found her boxing gloves about ten feet apart from each other on the other side of the bed. She frantically looked around for her robe, which wasn't on the floor. She glanced at Zach sleeping quietly and thought she made out something red on the dark bed. She got close enough to realize that it was in fact her robe and that Zach was curled up on it. She tried to tug it free, but quickly gave up on being gentle and gave it one last hard tug to wrest it free.

"What's going on?" he asked, rolling over off of her robe.

"Please tell me we just made out," Ariana begged.

"Nah, we had sex," Zach said. Tears rushed to Ariana's eyes but she quickly wiped them away.

"Okay," she said, "have a good night." She turned around and walked into the master bathroom to vomit again.

She did a good job of holding herself together until she got in Teddy's car. She silently listened to him make fun of her stumbling and her half-assed costume. When he asked her how her night had been though, she started crying uncontrollably.

"Hey, what happened?" he asked, concerned. He wondered if the few drunk jokes he had made a minute ago weren't appreciated by someone having their first bad experience with alcohol.

"I don't want to talk about it," she managed to eek out in between sobs.

"Okay, we'll talk in the morning," Teddy said.

"I don't want to talk about it," Ariana repeated. Teddy gave up asking and Ariana said nothing else the whole way home.

II

Part Two

9

A Long Way From Where We Were

The next morning, Nancy knocked on Ariana's door. She was dressed in grey workout leggings and a baggy pink t-shirt that had a ribbon on it for breast cancer awareness. She moved her feet from side to side as if warming up for her workout in advance. In reality, she was more nervous than anything else. Other than the brisk walks she had been taking since she had bought herself workout clothes, she hadn't exercised in six years. *What if I hurt myself? What if I jiggle too much in the mirror?* She promptly cut off her thoughts, trying instead to focus on the task at hand, which was getting Ariana out of bed. She knew that just being with her daughter would make her feel better. She knocked again, awaiting an answer.

"Ariana?" she called. "Are you awake?"

Ariana shifted from laying on her back to laying on her side. "Yeah. I'm not feeling so great though."

"Oh, honey what's wrong?"

"My stomach hurts," she said meekly. Ariana glanced at her phone that was on her bedside table. Nancy went to turn the knob to come in only to discover the door was locked.

"Honey, can I come in?"

"No, I don't want you to see me like this. I'll be fine, enjoy your Zumba class." Ariana rolled over onto her stomach and put her face in her pillow.

"Okay. If you're feeling better next week, do you want to go?"

She raised her head up from the pillow. "Yeah, sure." She plopped her head back down.

"Okay. Are you sure you don't need anything?"

"I'm good," she mumbled, her face still in the pillow.

"Okay. Feel better."

After Ariana heard Nancy go downstairs, she glanced at her phone again. Texts from Dan flooded the screen.

Hey, we need to talk about what happened with you and Zach last night, read the first message.

He followed up with, *So you'll sleep with anyone but me? Were you even a virgin? Or have you slept with half the school?*

Yes, I was a virgin. I wasn't planning on having sex with anyone, especially him, she responded. Then she decided another message was in order. *I'm sorry, okay, I was really drunk and he took me into the bedroom. I didn't know what was happening.*

Bullshit, you could have stopped it.

I froze, okay? I'm sorry, I don't know what else to say, she responded. Tears began to stream down her face and she buried her face in her pillow again and then picked her head up for a minute to type out one last text. *Listen, I feel awful about it. If I could undo it, I would. Trust me, I wish I could.*

I hope you know this means we're over, he said. Ariana felt a loud sob coming on and stuffed her face in her pillow to muffle it. As she cried over Dan, she suddenly realized that she wasn't as much upset about him breaking up with her as about what she had done. *How could I have let myself get so drunk? Now the whole school thinks I'm a slut and worse, I lost my virginity to my boyfriend's best friend.* She knew she would be ostracized come Monday and Zach would be getting high fives from the half of his friends that weren't also Dan's friends. *Ugh, why on earth did I have sex with him?* she thought. The worst part was that she couldn't even remember it. The feeling of melting into Zach's arms wasn't lingering as she tried to recreate the night in her mind and she sighed, wishing she could at least remember what it had felt like. She said a silent prayer that everyone would get the gossip out of their system this weekend and forget about the whole ordeal by the time Monday came around.

As Ariana turned the previous night over in her head, Nancy was downstairs making herself a smoothie. As she slowly sipped her spinach and strawberries, she reminded herself that working out again was going to be hard at first but that she had to start somewhere. She continued to give herself a silent pep talk as she got in the car and headed to her class. Once she got behind the wheel though, worries about Ariana started surfacing. She knew Ariana hadn't been doing well in school lately, as she had intercepted a progress report from one of her teachers. She had missed assignments in several different classes and was close to failing math. It was also unlike her to get sick in general, nevertheless fake being sick. She resolved to talk to her daughter when she returned from Zumba.

The first thing Nancy ended up doing after Zumba was vomiting though. She could hear the instructor calling to her from outside the bathroom. "I'm fine," she said. "Just really out of shape." She wretched again, tears flowing down her face. After she had rid her system of the smoothie, she walked back out to her car and cried for a few more minutes before drying her tears and pulling out. *Why did I ever stop moving?* she asked herself. She remembered training all the time only years ago. She couldn't entirely blame her injury either. She could have decided to go back and teach dance at the company, and maybe then she would have stayed in shape.

Then, Frank's words echoed through the past, "Welcome to the real world, Nancy. Get a real job that could actually help us pay the bills."

He was the one who had crushed her dreams. He had put the nail in the coffin when he reminded her that the kids would benefit from her having a "normal" job. It wasn't as if she was away from them often, but a couple weekends alone with them had been a few too many in Frank's book.

By the time she was done replaying the past in her head, she had arrived home. As she got out of the car, she tried to pull herself out of her problems and remember what she had wanted to do after Zumba. She showered and composed herself before approaching Ariana's door again. She knocked harder this time.

"Go away," was the automatic response. Ariana was now curled up in the fetal position, facing the wall.

"That's no way to talk to your mother," Nancy responded firmly.

"I don't want to be around anyone right now. I feel like shit."

"Can I come in? Maybe I can diagnose the problem," Nancy frowned and tapped lightly on the door with her long fingernails.

"No."

Nancy glanced down the hall in both directions and lowered her voice. The image of her daughter carrying a Victoria's secret bag the other day had been plaguing her since the car ride home from the mall and she was terrified that she had failed as a mother for not having talked to her daughter about safe sex.

"Ariana, if I ask you a serious question will you answer it?"

"Maybe."

"Are you pregnant?"

"Eww no! Mom why would you think that?" After the words left her mouth though, the sinking realization that she could be set in. She felt a wave of nausea rise and wondered if it was possible that she wasn't hangover, but suffering from morning sickness.

"Because you're complaining about nausea early in the morning and you're not doing well in school. Honey, we need to talk."

"Mom, I'm not pregnant. I'm 90% sure it's the stomach flu."

"Okay. Just remember that it's really hard to hide a baby," Nancy said, walking down the hall to her room. She settled down on her bed, grabbed her laptop from the bedside table, and started looking up ways to talk to one's daughter about sex.

Teddy, who had heard part of Nancy and Ariana's conversation from his room, got up out of bed and knocked on Ariana's door.

"Go away, Mom!" Ariana yelled.

"It's me, Teddy."

"Go away!" she repeated.

Teddy tried her doorknob, but it was locked. He knew that his parents kept the key above their door frame, so he walked over toward their door, reached up, and grabbed the key. He opened Ariana's door and she shrieked at him. He quickly locked the door behind him so his mother wouldn't come rushing in.

"What the fuck Teddy, I said go away!" she screamed, bolting upright in bed.

"What the hell happened last night?"

"I don't want to talk about it."

"Ariana, I picked you up from a house in the middle of nowhere last night, no questions asked, lied to mom for you, and put you to bed when we got home. If anyone deserves an explanation this morning, it's me." He looked into her bloodshot eyes and softened his voice. "Was it that party that mom banned you from?"

"Yes," Ariana said tersely.

"Okay, there's a start. Can you please tell me what happened? I know you got really drunk but that's about it."

"I told you that?" she asked.

"No, but you almost vomited in my car. I had to pull over so you could vomit on the side of the road. I made you drink a whole bottle of water when you got home," he said, pointing to the empty water bottle on her bedside table.

Ariana racked her brain, but couldn't recall that part of the night. She remembered waking up, finding out she slept with Zach, and calling Teddy to give her a ride home. She didn't remember much before or after the crucial realization that she had lost her virginity, and even then she might have been able to convince herself it had been a dream if Dan hadn't texted her.

"What's on your face?" Teddy said, pointing to her upper lip. Ariana stood up to look in the mirror and saw something red and crusty stuck to her upper lip. She brushed it off and it fell into the palm of her hand.

"Looks like pizza sauce," she said, confused.

"Oh, it must be from the pizza bagels last night."

"What pizza bagels?"

"I made us pizza bagels last night. You know, to soak up the booze."

"Wow, I don't remember that at all. Thanks, I guess." Ariana looked away, embarrassed that the brother who could barely take care of himself had managed to take care of her.

"Wait, were you high when you picked me up last night?" she asked, looking up at him again.

"I was sober enough to drive and make sure you

were okay," he said, trying to read the emotion in her eyes. He could discern sadness, and maybe a little guilt, but he wasn't entirely sure. He could tell that she was far from ready to talk about it though, so instead of continuing to press the subject, he let himself out and locked the door behind him.

10

Lazy Sunday

After isolating herself all day on Saturday, Ariana felt it was about time to leave the house. She decided to respond to the texts she had originally ignored from Kelsey by suggesting they go to the mall.

When Kelsey picked Ariana up and immediately asked what happened the previous night, Ariana didn't know how to respond. She was silent for a moment as she ran through three different lead-ins in her head. The first involved her simply saying she had sex with Zach, which was the truth, but wasn't exactly authentic to the way things had happened. The second involved her saying she had gotten too drunk to function and had blacked out, which was also accurate but made it seem like she took no responsibility for her actions. The third forced her to admit that she had probably had some sober desire to sabotage her relationship to begin with and therefore her drunk self hadn't had the self-control to say no. She knew that the last option was probably the most truthful, but she knew that Kelsey might misinterpret "sober desire" to directly correlate to cheating when it in fact just referred to general sabotage. She had come pretty close to accusing Dan of cheating on her with Marcy the other night, so she had imagined that would have been what would have caused him to break up with her. After her mental gymnastics, she decided to go with option two because she reasoned that teenagers never took responsibility, especially when alcohol was involved.

"You don't remember losing your virginity?" Kelsey practically screamed as Ariana tried to explain, "Where was I?"

"I don't know, I was trying to find you all night. Did you leave with Dan?"

"No, he left early. I don't think Marcy was feeling well so he took her home."

Ariana grimaced and fought the urge to make a comment about how he had probably been sleeping with Marcy when she had been sleeping with Zach, but refrained. She had a feeling that Dan would make everything look like it was her fault no matter what she said.

"Did you guys use a condom?" Kelsey asked as she turned into the mall parking lot.

"I can't remember," Ariana sighed, "if I was sober,

I know I would've thought about it."

Silence fell over the car as the weight of Ariana's comment hung in the air.

"But then again, I also wouldn't have had sex with him in the first place," Ariana said, swinging her purse over her shoulder and stepping out of Kelsey's car. Kelsey followed suit and the two girls entered the mall.

"You should probably get a pregnancy test," Kelsey said as they walked past the mall's CVS.

"Yeah, I should," Ariana said. The two girls turned around and walked into the store. She felt ashamed checking out with a pregnancy test and prayed her period would come on time so she wouldn't have to use it.

* * *

Frank sauntered into the living around six that night to find Nancy watching Dateline. He approached her stiffly, trying to hide his aggravation. He had just come back from visiting his father in the nursing home and was exhausted. Upon seeing how relaxed she was, he decided that he had a worse day than her and that he was the one who deserved to relax. He didn't sit down immediately, but instead hovered over her.

"How was your day?"

"Pretty good. How was yours?"

He took a deep breath. "It was alright. What'd you do today?" he asked, grimacing at the TV.

"I went for a walk this morning and went shopping after I dropped Ariana off at dance. Her teacher and I had a chat about her pursuing dance as a career."

"Is that really a good idea though?" he said. "It's a career that relies on your body to be in tip-top shape and it's so easy to get injured."

"Well she's still going to go to college and get a degree as a back-up plan. My injury was so crushing because I didn't have a real back-up plan. I may have gotten a degree in history but I never thought about how I might use it" She glanced back at the TV to shake her memory of regret.

"Still," he said. Nancy rolled her eyes and turned her attention back to the TV.

Frank realized that she was engrossed in the show and tried to break her focus.

"I had a really rough day at Dad's," he said.

"Really? How's he doing?" she asked, her eyes still glued to the television.

"Not good. He's losing it. He had a bad day today. Asked me if I was from Ukraine."

"I'm sorry," she said, looking away from the TV and right at him. She rose and hugged him, trying to ignite some sort of empathy for him. He half-hugged her, placing his hands ever so lightly on the small of her back.

"It's okay," he said, pulling away. "I lost him a long time ago. It's just horrible to watch."

"Yeah. I don't ever want to be a burden on you like that." Nancy glanced down at her stomach and reconsidered watching TV for much longer.

"Why would you?" he asked, glancing down at the TV guide on the end table.

Nancy clasped her hand over her mouth and tried to fight back tears. "Because I'm fat. I don't want to die of a heart attack and leave you with the kids."

More like leave the kids with you, she thought to herself, trying to turn her tears into anger. It was this thought that made her cry more than the sentiment she had expressed out loud.

"Don't say that," he said half-heartedly. He suddenly remembered how easy it used to be to feign emotion and realized that it was getting harder.

"But it could happen," she said between sobs, "That's why I'm trying to exercise and eat better. I want to be healthy again." She hugged him again and he pulled away after a few seconds, saying he had to shower.

After Frank left the room, Nancy sat back down on the couch and told herself that she had earned some time to relax. She was beginning to make progress on being more active and was doing well at her new job.

She eased back into a reclined position and started to fall asleep.

11

Family Dinner

When Frank reached his office on Monday after driving his wife into work for the second time, he was still reeling from his encounter with Isabelle on Friday. It had almost seemed like a sneak attack. *Maybe Isabelle recognized my car?* he wondered. *Or did Nancy find out and plan the whole thing out?* He had noticed that she hadn't been talking to him nearly as much recently and knew that she had been ignoring him when he was trying to talk to her the previous night.

Frank impulsively reached into his pocket to grab his phone, started typing a text to Nancy, and promptly stopped himself. He backspaced the message text and texted Andy instead. He asked Andy if he should be honest with his wife and set his phone down on his desk. He glanced over at the pile of four or five accordion files that lay to the left of his desk and put his face in his hands.

How am I supposed to work like this? he thought. He gave himself a few minutes to wait for Andy to respond and when his response didn't come right away, Frank leaned back in his chair to try to relax for a few minutes, closed his eyes, and fell asleep.

Frank hadn't even realized he had fallen asleep until he heard his phone ringing. When he picked up his phone to answer Andy's call, he realized that it was a little after noon.

"Shit!" he cursed to himself. He accepted the call and after the two men exchanged pleasantries, asked, "So what do you think I should do?"

"Well first of all, why do you think she knows? Are you sure you're not just being paranoid?"

"Positive. Nancy just got a job at the same company where Isabelle works. If she wasn't suspicious before, she definitely is now because Isabelle saw me dropping her off on Friday."

"Are you sure she saw you?"

"She came over and said hi," Frank said through gritted teeth. He began sifting through the pile of files on his desk.

"Oh shit! Okay, honestly, Nancy's probably already knows. I would suck up if I were you. You know, get on her good side."

Frank grimaced at the thought as he pulled the file

he was looking for out of the stack on his desk. He balanced the phone between his shoulder and his ear to make it easier to multitask.

"Ugh, you think? I was hoping you'd say I was wrong and that stuff like this only happens in movies."

Andy sighed. "Brace yourself man. Best thing you can do is get home before her and cook or clean. Women love when you do that."

"You know, that's not a horrible idea. I have to be in court at 1:30. Maybe I'll just head home afterwards."

"Sounds like a plan. I'm gonna eat lunch now but let me know how it goes."

"Thanks, will do." Frank hung up the phone, dropped it on his desk, and began delving into the file he had pulled. He had to meet his client in court in 45 minutes.

* * *

Nancy was surprised to come home to Frank cooking dinner when she got home that evening.

"What are you doing home?" she asked.

"Just figured I'd make some dinner," he said. He smiled at her and then turned his back to her to tend to the scallops on the stove. The whole house smelled like seafood and Nancy plugged her nose.

"Well, that, umm, will be quite a dinner. Why on earth are you cooking scallops? Didn't we establish that they make the house reek?"

"Because we haven't eaten seafood in a while. I thought they were one of your favorites?" Frank asked, gulping a bit. Remnants of this previous discussion were beginning to flood into the forefront of his mind.

"Only when I eat out. I don't cook them because they smell," she said, taking her coat off and hanging it over a kitchen chair. She set her purse down on the chair and fished out her phone. She checked the time to find that it was only 5:30.

"How'd you get out of work so early?" she asked, setting her phone down on the table. He suddenly remembered that his wife's car was still in the shop and that she hadn't even texted him asking for a ride home.

"Well, that case that's been killing me went to court this afternoon and finally settled so that nightmare is mostly over. After that, I took the rest of the day off and figured I'd do some stuff around the house to help you out now that you have a new job and all."

"Aww, that's nice of you," she said.

"Wait, how did you get home?" he asked.

"Oh, Isabelle, that woman you met on Friday

morning offered to drive me home," she said, "What a sweet girl." She smiled to herself when she saw Frank's spine become rigid and his movements stiffen.

"Why would you go home with her?" Frank half yelled. He could feel his heart beating faster and reminded himself to calm down.

"You know, you could have just called me to come get you," he said in a quieter voice.

"Oh, I didn't want to bother you at work. Besides, she said she only lives ten minutes away from here."

"Really?" His heart sped up yet again. He didn't remember his drive home being particularly short and wondered if Nancy was trying to pull a fast one on him.

"Yeah, she actually offered to pick me up and drop me off until my car gets out of the shop on Wednesday so that you don't have to." Nancy didn't mention that the car ride home had been awkward at best and that she was scared that tomorrow's ride in would be just as painful.

"That's great," Frank said, turning around to hide his grimace. *She either really doesn't want to risk seeing me again or wants to know where I live so she can kill me in my sleep,* he thought.

He flipped the scallops over, revealing a golden-brown sear and yelled, "Dinner's almost ready!"

"Where's the veggies?" Nancy asked, seeing nothing but an empty package of scallops on the counter behind her husband.

"Oh crap, I forgot," he said. "Can you make a salad or something really quick?"

"Sure," Nancy said. She wasn't sure if her husband knew she knew about his affair or if he had miraculously become a different man, but either way, she didn't complain.

Maybe I shouldn't let on that I know something's up. Maybe he'll keep making dinner and cleaning the house, she thought as she walked over to the fridge and tore open a bag of spinach. She bent down to grab a bowl out of a cabinet. She stood up, dumped the spinach in the bowl, and searched the fridge for other salad ingredients. She found shredded carrots, Craisins, walnuts, and part of a log of goat cheese. She tossed the salad together and carried the bowl to the table right as Ariana emerged from the stairway.

"Can you help set the table?" Nancy asked her with a tired smile. Ariana agreed to help and followed her mother back into the kitchen to grab plates and silverware.

Nancy brought two different salad dressings to the table and walked over to the stairs after she set them down.

"Teddy, dinner's ready!" she yelled.

"He's not here," Ariana said as she set the third (and last) plate down at the table.

"Then where is he?" Nancy demanded, startling herself with how quickly her tone had changed.

"He said he went to Dexter's for dinner."

Ariana winced as she heard her dad slam his hand into the counter behind her. "Damn it, what did we do wrong with that boy? Didn't we raise him to have respect for his parents? That boy is never home for dinner."

"Maybe he forgot," Nancy said. The knowledge that her husband was the reason her son was never home made her voice go soft and she suddenly felt sympathetic towards Teddy. She wished she had a place to escape to when her husband became unbearable.

"He forgot he has to eat? No, he just wants to piss me off. God, I can't stand the kid."

"Have you ever thought that maybe he can't stand you?" Ariana cut in. "You're always telling him that he used to be such a good student, that he used to be great at soccer. You know why you say 'used to'? It's because you pushed him too hard towards goals that weren't his own. I'd leave too if I were him. We're both sick of you. It's too much pressure to live up to your unrealistic expectations."

"Don't talk to me like that," he yelled, his face getting red. "I work hard every single day so you can have a roof over your head, buy nice clothes, and afford to take dance lessons. You owe me."

Ariana, already fed up with the gossip she had heard in the hallways that day, lost it. "I may owe you money, but I don't owe you love!" she screamed. She ran upstairs into her room and locked her door. She collapsed onto her bed and cried. She remembered when she was little and used to worship her dad because he used to teach her sports. He used to make her feel strong. The older she got though, the more she felt like the father she knew when she was a child didn't exist anymore.

He used to try to teach her how to play soccer with him and Teddy, but she wasn't great at it. She didn't have much eye-foot coordination, so he put her on defense. He used to call her the "impenetrable wall", but when Teddy got recruited by a travel team when he was twelve, she was no longer invited to practice with him and her dad. She was only eight when she learned her place in her family. That was when she got bored, stumbled across her mom's dance videos, and started to take the dance classes she was already enrolled in more seriously.

Her mother had always been supportive of her though, and Ariana was grateful for that. She was the one who drove her to dance and who dressed up to see her perform at her recitals. As she realized that Teddy had stopped playing soccer six years ago, she wondered what her father's most recent excuse for not showing up to her recitals would be.

She remembered that Teddy had also been a different person years ago. He and Ariana used to have a great relationship and now they barely talked. She didn't know why he was always hanging out with Dexter, but she assumed it was because he didn't want to come home and face their father. She didn't think that Teddy smoked weed to piss her dad off as much as he wanted to think that was the case; she thought that he smoked weed to escape the pressure her father had created for him. It wasn't like he ever did anything malicious towards anyone who didn't deserve it.

He never had a problem dishing it out to someone who did deserve it though. She remembered being in fourth grade and getting made fun of by Billy Gordon, the biggest bully in school. He was a fifth grader who started picking on all the girls in Ariana's grade after he had finished with the girls in his grade. He used to make fun of her teeth, saying that she reminded him of a rabbit because she had buckteeth. She remembered crying in her room one day after school when Teddy walked by and asked her what was wrong. She had told him the whole story and the next day, Billy Gordon came into school with a black eye. Rumors flew, and kids started saying that the two boys had gotten into fight on the playground. Ariana had asked Teddy what had really happened, and was disappointed to hear that it wasn't as eventful as her classmates had made it sound. There had been no, "Meet me on the playground," banter, just a punch thrown in passing at Billy's expense. Nevertheless, she kind of liked the story that made her brother sound cool, so she didn't make any effort to disprove the rumors.

Her thoughts continued moving like a movie reel and an image of her and Teddy running around their backyard when they were little flashed through her mind. She remembered that they used to play hide and seek tag all the time. She remembered hiding in the dryer, where Teddy was never able to find her. She would usually be discovered when Nancy would go to do laundry. She would scream that Ariana was going to get hurt, and Ariana would hide in the backyard instead.

"I was just here ten minutes ago," he would say, "and I can see half of you from behind that tree."

"Maybe I'm a ghost," she used to joke, not wanting to give up her true hiding place. Now when she opened the dryer, she would sometimes find small plastic baggies that had accidentally gone through the wash. She supposed it was a good thing that they always smelled of weed and never had a white residue, but was still frustrated that Teddy smoked all the time. She had a feeling Teddy was smart enough not to leave more incriminating evidence behind (like the drug itself), but either way, he was lucky that she had been doing the laundry lately and not their mother.

Ariana mused about the past for hours that night, ignoring her hunger completely. She laid down on her bed and began to fall herself falling further and further down, until she was almost cocooning inside of herself. She fell asleep with the lights on and had to get up to turn them off at one in the morning.

12

Slut Shaming

Ariana's alarm sounded at 6:30 in the morning and she begrudgingly got up and went to school. She moved slowly, hoping that if she could drag out the time she wouldn't have to endure another day of Dan ignoring her every time she tried to make eye contact or approach him. She knew that he loved spreading rumors, so when she finally arrived at school and saw Marcy and Anna huddled around Dan at his locker, she felt as though she was doomed to an infamous existence for the rest of high school. They all shot sideways glances at her as she walked down the hall but she proceeded to her locker, which was inconveniently opposite his. She knew they were whispering about her but pretended she didn't notice. She slung her backpack to the ground and opened her locker slowly. She could feel tears beginning to well up in her eyes and looked down at her backpack to avoid being seen. She picked each book out of her backpack individually and methodically lined the books up on the top shelf of her locker. She then began to rearrange the books by color, hoping that organizing would help her calm down. She took a few breaths and glanced back at Dan's locker. When she saw that he and his friends were gone, she breathed a small sigh of relief and hung her back pack up in her locker. She grabbed her history and math books, shut her locker, and walked towards her homeroom.

When she arrived, she saw Kelsey sitting in her usual spot in the far right corner of the room, near the door. The girls waved to each other and Ariana sat down next to Kelsey.

"How're you doing?" Kelsey asked, twirling a piece of her dirty blond hair around her finger. She was balancing one leg on the desk and precariously leaning back in her chair.

"Eh, I've been better. I saw Marcy and Anna talking to Dan about me in the hallway."

Kelsey slammed her chair on the ground and turned towards Ariana. "That doesn't surprise me. Did I not tell you that they're major bitches when you started hanging out with them? When I started dating David they were super fake nice to me then told the whole school that David was my beard. Do you not remember that?"

"Yeah, I guess you warned me," Ariana said, looking down and adjusting her books so that they lined up evenly.

"I just hate this whole thing. Why are people making such a big deal out of it? Even if I cheated when I was stone cold sober, guys do it all the time."

"Key word: guys. Also, people think it was intentional. I mean, it was his best friend, how could you not?"

Ariana felt like she had been punched in the stomach and was ready to retaliate. "Kels, do you think I meant to sleep with Zach the other night?" she asked in a low voice.

Sensing Ariana's anger, Kelsey quickly changed her tone. "No, I believe you. I was there. You were absolutely shit faced. Even if you did have the hots for him, you were both so drunk that any sex wasn't technically consensual. I wouldn't call it rape, but I wouldn't call it cheating either."

Ariana's wave of nausea passed and she caught her breath again. "Okay, I'm glad you understand," she said, looking Kelsey in the eye.

"I'm just saying," Kelsey said, "people are going to believe what they want to believe." The homeroom bell rang and the two girls exchanged rushed goodbyes as they exited the classroom and filed into the sea of students in the hallway. Ariana was swept off to her math class and Kelsey headed the opposite direction.

Ariana walked through the hallways with her head down, her long hair creating a shield between her and the rest of the school. She was dreading going to math for many reasons, and the fact that she shared the class with Dan was one of them. She heard his booming voice before she even walked into the classroom, so she didn't look up as she walked through the door. She went directly to the back of the room but stayed in the column of desks closest to the door so as to make her escape that much easier. She sat down, set her books down on her desk, and pretended to examine the cover of her math book while listening to what was happening around her. She could hear Dan talking about baseball with his friends and felt a rush of sadness and anger wash over her. She was sad that she wouldn't hear his enthusiasm again but angry that he was pretending that everything was fine. His life wasn't ruined. If anything, he would have more girls flocking him than ever before because they thought he was a victim of infidelity and wanted to offer him a shoulder to cry on. Ariana was glad she hadn't actually seen that, but she had overheard girls in the bathroom saying that they felt "horrible for him" because he had been dating "such a slut". She had hid in the bathroom a lot the previous day to avoid Marcy and Anna, who sneered at her every time they saw her and who seemed to spend more time wandering the halls than in class.

Ariana spent all class trying to focus, but to no avail. She kept thinking about the conversations she had overheard in the last day, how many times she had walked into a room and the crowd had begun to fall silent, and how many times she had wanted to punch Dan for ignoring her. She couldn't handle it. Not only did she already feel like a horrible person, but she knew that she was on the verge of lashing out like one. By the time she had replayed yesterday's trauma of everyone stopping and staring at her during lunch for the third time in her head, the bell rang. She quickly gathered her things so that she could beat Dan out the door, but her teacher, Mr. Balley, called her over.

Ariana walked over like a stiff puppet being tugged on a string and asked him what he wanted.

"You seem a little off today," he said, "Is everything okay?"

"Yeah," she lied, looking down and covering her face with her hair.

"Listen, I know high school can be tough. The guys over there don't exactly make it easy to focus," he said, pointing to the window seats where Dan and his friends sat.

"Yeah," she said, glancing up. *Oh God, do all the teachers know what I did too?* she wondered. She shifted her weight from her left foot to her right.

"But you are falling behind in this class, and have been for quite some time." He paused, glancing down at the copy of the statistics book on his desk. "I'll tell you what: you hand in all your missing homework assignments in the next two weeks and I won't fail you for the semester."

"Okay, thank you."

"And I can help you out if you come to me for math help in the morning," he said with a small smile.

Ariana looked up, shocked by his kindness. He was the first person who had been reasonable with her in the past seventy-two hours and she wanted to throw her arms around him and hug him. Instead, she gave him a sad smile and thanked him before walking off to her next class.

She managed to focus better in history, her favorite subject. She felt better about her chances of getting into college now that she knew she wouldn't fail math her senior year. She was also glad that the only class she shared with Dan was over for the day.

Her high of the day quickly became a low when she went to return her books to her locker after history and found the word "SLUT" drawn in thick black letters on her red locker. She tried to rub part of the "T" off, but it stuck. She felt her eyes becoming wet but quickly channeled her sadness into anger. She knew that this wasn't a random attack and that Dan's friends, Marcy and Anna, were most definitely the instigators. As more students began to fill the halls behind her, Ariana turned around and searched the block of lockers across from her to see if she could find Dan. As the crowd began to thin, she spotted Dan at his locker. Surprisingly, he was alone. She decided to take advantage of his vulnerability. She loaded her backpack with all the books she needed for the night and shut her locker. She dropped her backpack in front of her locker and stormed across the hallway to Dan. He glanced at her quickly, then looked away, ignoring her. He placed a book in his locker and she slammed it shut.

"Why are you ignoring me and spreading rumors when you know I was drunk off my ass and wouldn't dream of doing something like that sober? I get if you're pissed at me because I'm pissed at me, but have the decency to keep it between us instead of telling the whole fucking school."

Dan responded by looking at her with a stupefied expression.

"I didn't want to have sex with your best friend, okay?" she continued. "I was drunk and he was drunk and we made a mistake. You were there, you saw how sloshed I was."

His expression shifted from dumbfounded to angry as he realized that the people nearby were listening in on their conversation. He began to enter his locker combination again in an effort to look inconspicuous.

"I don't care how drunk you were," he whispered harshly, "you had sex with my best friend after telling me you weren't 'ready for sex yet'. And you had the balls to start dancing with him right in front of me, not to mention the entire team? We're done."

"But I didn't want to have sex with him! I was so drunk I didn't know what I wanted," Ariana yelled, counteracting his quiet anger. The other students in Dan's locker block fell quiet. Ariana could feel everyone's eyes on her and knew she had to say something that would make her seem sympathetic but not desperate. "I'm sorry I slept with Zach but I'm not sorry we broke up!" she yelled.

He paused as he lifted his political science textbook out of his locker and looked at her with his brown eyes. She couldn't see an ounce of pain in them, not a hint of sadness mingled with his hatred. She slammed his locker shut again, forcing him to enter his combination for the third time, and walked away. She picked up her backpack and went to the locker room to join the gym class that was going outside to play tennis. She walked outside with them and began the twenty-minute walk home.

As she walked home with tears streaming down her face, she thought back to how different Dan had been when they first met. They had been sophomores, and he had been on the JV baseball team. He had seemed like a goofy guy with his shaggy brown hair and eyes that were so blue she wanted to swim in them. She remembered staring into those eyes on their first date. She had felt like she was in a movie when after dinner, he asked her if she wanted to stargaze in the bed of his dad's truck. She had said yes and had thought that he was too good to be true. Their whole relationship felt like a dream now that she was experiencing who he really was with lucidity for the first time.

But she could also look back and see the signs that she missed. He had been a different person when they met. He used to make fun of the jocks and call them douchebags, but now she was wondering if that was because he had been jealous of them, not because he had genuinely disliked their behavior. He used to go to church all the time when they first met and when she told him she wasn't religious, he had said that it didn't matter as long as she was a good person who was capable of forgiveness.

"That's the most important part of the New Testament anyway," he had said. She didn't know if it was his rigorous training program that had turned him into a star athlete and stripped away his humbleness or if it was his parent's messy divorce that had made him lose his faith and belief in forgiveness, but either way, he most definitely wasn't the boy she had met two years ago.

* * *

Ariana was surprised to see Teddy at home when she got home at eleven. She walked through the front door to find him channel surfing in sweats, the remote in his right hand and his left hand in his pants. Upon hearing the door close, he quickly shifted his left hand onto his stomach.

"What are you doing home?" he asked, upset that his alone time was being ruined.

"I can ask you the same question," she said defensively, trying her hardest not to breakdown in front of Teddy for the second time in two weeks.

"If you must know, I can't live at Dexter's forever. I do need time alone to unwind."

Ariana rolled her eyes. "Please, your life revolves around getting high. How much more unwound can you get?"

"You're just mad because I bailed on the family dinner last night."

"Yeah, I am," she said, dropping her backpack to the ground and channeling her anger at Dan towards her brother. "You left me alone with the crazy. Dad went on one of his rants again. I tried to stand up for you but I don't think it worked." She gulped back more tears.

"I doubt it. Thanks for trying though." He looked his sister up and down, trying to assess what else was wrong. "You skipping school to protest him?"

"No," she said. She walked closer and sat down on

the couch next to him. "What are you watching?"

He sensed her stiffness and decided not to press the subject. *Maybe it has something to do with that party*, he thought. He knew the feeling of people giving him a hard time, so didn't want to press his sister at the moment. He was sick of Dexter giving him a hard time about always being at his place and not paying rent. He remembered telling him that he was trying to get a job and get his own place even though he wasn't. If he had been smart, he would've saved up all the money his dad randomly gave him when he was younger and put it towards moving out. *Maybe that's what he wanted*, Teddy thought to himself, *maybe all those Andrew Jackson's were a subtle hint to get out.* He cringed when he realized that he had spent most, if not all, of those spare twenties on weed. *I need a time machine*, he thought to himself as Ariana curled into a ball and fell asleep on the couch next to him.

* * *

Frank was having similar thoughts in his downtown office, but for different reasons. *Of course I have to slip up with someone my wife works with. Why couldn't there have been anyone else in the bar?* He wasn't sure if he was acting out of guilt or fear when he picked up the phone to text her, but, per usual he didn't take the time to figure it out. He simply asked her to not say anything to his wife about the affair and waited for a response for about five minutes before going back to work.

When he checked his phone again at the end of the day, she still hadn't responded. He rationalized the silence by telling himself that she was probably working late. He managed to convince himself of this fact so much that he was shocked when he got home and saw that his wife was eating take out at the kitchen table.

"You're home already?" he said, taking his coat off and hanging it up on the back of a kitchen chair.

"Why wouldn't I be? It's six o'clock" she asked, hesitantly putting her fork in her questionable Chinese chicken. She nodded to the Chinese takeout on counter with a full mouth. "There's some for you if you want," she said after she finished chewing.

Frank felt his heart jump up to his throat and tried to swallow it back down. "Oh, I just figured that with Isabelle being a higher up and all, you'd be stuck there later as she finished up her work for the day."

"No, she finishes at 5 like the rest of us. And how did you know her name?" she asked, trying to poke holes in the story that she knew was about to fall apart any minute.

Frank loosened his tie, hoping that would help him swallow the lump in his throat. "You introduced us the other day, remember?"

"Oh right," Nancy said, taking a bite of her chicken and raising her eyes to Frank's, "I must have forgotten."

He gulped. Her stare was kind and suspicious at the same time, as only a mother's could be. He used to love watching his kids squirm like a worm under a microscope when the light of her green eyes penetrated theirs but now he was the one who felt like an insect that was about to be dissected. He didn't know exactly what he was afraid of. He didn't think that anything bad would happen between the two of them in the long run if she found out. He didn't think she would divorce him, or even yell at him. He was avoiding the truth because he was scared of living in a passive aggressive household for the rest of his life. *Isn't that marriage though?* he thought to himself. *Isn't that what I'm already doing?*

He broke her stare by telling her he had to go upstairs to change out of his work clothes. When he walked into their bedroom, he laid down on their bed and took a few deep breaths. He comforted himself in the fact that Nancy was too timid to actually confront him and then got up and walked into the walk-in-closet to change into more comfortable clothes. When he came back downstairs, Ariana was talking with her mother at the kitchen table. He could hear bits and pieces of the conversation as he rounded the corner to the dining room. He could tell they were talking about college and a wave of excitement washed over him. He was thrilled that they would soon have one less kid in the house.

"But Brandeis is so expensive," Nancy said. Frank's excitement was suddenly dampened by the price of having one of his children out of the house.

Maybe I can convince her to commute, he thought. He walked into the kitchen and pretended to be looking for something as he listened in on their conversation. He started by opening the cabinets to the far left, where the dishes were, and slowly made his way over to the right. He heard Ariana mention UCLA, Duke, and Fordham within the two-minute time frame that he was banging around in the cabinets. He heard Nancy complaining that those schools were too far away and that she needed to stay around Connecticut, or at least New England. She protested that Fordham wasn't that far and then her mother argued that it was too expensive.

Nancy was trying to stay focused on the conversation she was having with her daughter, but her husband's rustling around was starting to annoy her.

If I hear one more cabinet door slam, she thought as Ariana began to launch into her diatribe about how awful New England was and how awful it would be to commute because she would end up going to college with everyone from high school. Nancy interrupted her when Frank slammed another cabinet closed.

Nancy turned around in her chair and looked at her husband. "Jesus Frank, what on earth are you looking for?"

"My mother's bowl," he lied. He had already opened that cabinet twice in his "search".

"It's in the far-left cabinet," she said, sighing. She turned back to face her daughter.

"Sorry, Ari. We'll talk about college some other time." Nancy hoisted herself up out of her seat and walked towards the kitchen. Frank had placed the bowl on the counter and had put lettuce in it while Nancy and Ariana had been talking. He was rummaging through their vegetable drawers when Nancy walked into the kitchen.

"But Mom, early decision applications are due soon!"

"We'll talk about it after dinner. I need to help your father make food first though."

"Ugh, fine," Ariana said, rolling her eyes. She stood up and walked upstairs towards her room. "Let me know when dinner's ready," she said as she began to ascend the stairs.

When she got to her room, she closed and locked her door. She sat down at her desk, opened her laptop, and continued filling out the Common Application for college. She stared at the list of colleges she had written on a sticky note near the mouse pad on her laptop and began typing them into Common App's search engine. When she finally finished, she felt satisfied that she would get into at least three of the schools she was applying to. She had added Fordham, Brandeis, UCLA, Duke, Tufts and the University of Pennsylvania to her current list of LSU, Notre Dame, and Simmons. She then minimized the application and opened up a Word document entitled "College Essay". She read over what she had already written and crossed it out.

~~I wish I could stay more positive. Some days I think I can make it through and other days I just want to give up and go to bed. Half the time I want to sleep the day away but the sun harasses me, shining in my eyes and reminding me that there are things that need to be done regardless of how much I don't want to do them. The moon beckons me back to sleep, back to a dark lull where I can inhabit another body, another life in my dream world.~~

She couldn't remember why she had begun with what sounded like a diary entry. She tried racking her brain to figure out how she was going to stand out to these schools. She began typing:

I always wondered why my parents expected my brother and I to be perfect. Maybe it's because they both strove for perfection. A famous dancer and a lawyer. Talk about power couple. My mom doesn't dance anymore because she tore her Achilles tendon a few years back, but my dad's still a lawyer. Now he's just one that's tired and old. I guess the glory days wore off. Maybe that's why they put so much pressure on me and Teddy. Too bad we both let them down.

She hit the space bar a few times and then jotted down an idea:

Talk about Teddy and how I want to make a change and help people- psych program? She leaned back in her desk chair, looking at what she had written. She wondered if she could write a convincing essay about Teddy when she had such mixed feelings towards him. They had been close when they were kids, but ever since he met Dexter, he had been distant. Ariana was still a little bitter about this, but considered that he seemed to be caring about her a little more than usual lately and so tried to avoid writing anything negative for the time being.

She felt like she owed him something for picking her up from that dreadful party last week. She had had a full-on mental breakdown and he hadn't pushed the subject that night. Granted, he tried to figure it out the next morning, but Ariana wasn't entirely sure she could blame him for that. Even though she had lashed out on him at the time, she knew he was justified in asking her what had happened. She sat upright in her chair and grabbed the journal to the left of her laptop. She closed her laptop, placed the journal on top of it, and began writing.

Maybe we're never totally alone in our darkest moments. What if we just create that space for ourselves because it feels safer to be alone? Teddy was physically there for me. Maybe he would have listened to me if I had let him.

Ariana dropped her pen, unsure of how she wanted to proceed. She re-read what she had just written, picked the pen up to write again, and thought for a minute. Unable to fully articulate the passing thought she had, she put the pen down, closed her journal, and got up from her desk. She laid down on her bed and checked her phone. As she scrolled through Facebook, she saw pictures of Marcy and Anna at the mall and found old pictures of them at the pool over the summer, their hair perfectly coiffed as they tanned their already tan bodies. Ariana saw that Dan was tagged with them and that Marcy had given him photo credits in the post. Suddenly overcome by jealousy, she clicked on his name and went to his page. She scrolled down but realized that she couldn't see the most recent photos of Marcy and Anna on his timeline. She scrolled back up to the top to see if she missed something, and when she scrolled up to his profile picture, she saw the option to add him as a friend.

"That bastard!" she whispered loudly to herself. She then clicked on his "About" section and saw that he was officially dating Marcy. "Motherfucker," she whispered. She put her phone face down on her bedside table and walked over to the collage of pictures she had hanging on her door. She ripped off every picture with either him or Marcy and threw them in the trash. She collapsed onto her bed and cried for half an hour before she remembered her homework and Mr. Balley's promise to her. She sat at her desk and tried to channel her anger into her math homework, but it was no use. She decided to confront Dan the next morning and go for math help after she had unleashed her wrath.

13

Chinese Finger Traps

Unfortunately, Dan wasn't at his locker when she reached hers the next morning, so she just went straight to the school's tutoring center for extra help. Mr. Balley was glad to see her and told her that she was beginning to get the hang of it as they walked out of the tutoring center and to his class. He made math jokes with her to fill the otherwise awkward silence and she provided forced laughter. As they walked into the classroom, she saw Dan staring and blushed, ashamed that she had needed to get extra help from her teacher. She stopped laughing and put her head down as she walked to her desk. She sat in the same seat she had the day before, next to the girl whose dreads reeked of sweat and weed. She was quiet too, and one of the smarter girls in their remedial math class. They had exchanged small talk previously, but not in the past week. To distract herself from Dan's glare, she said hi to the girl and they began chatting about the homework. As they were in the middle of talking about factorials, Dan sauntered over and stood behind Ariana. The girl nodded her head to signal that someone was behind Ariana and she stopped talking. Sensing his looming presence, she held her breath and didn't turn around. He bent down and whispered in her ear.

"What were you and Mr. Balley talking about that's so funny? Are you fucking the teachers now too?"

Her face flushed red but she didn't turn around and give him the satisfaction of knowing that he had upset her. She glanced towards the girl with the dreads and saw her conceal a smile. Ariana suddenly realized how ridiculous Dan's accusation was and wondered if maybe she was taking the wrong approach to dealing with him.

"Yeah," she whispered sarcastically, biting her lower lip to keep from laughing. "He's the next most eligible bachelor on my list."

The girl with the dreads snorted to suppress a laugh and Ariana couldn't help but laugh a little too.

"Dan," the girl with the dreads began, turning around in her seat to face him, "who on earth would want to have sex with Mr. Balley?"

Dan shrugged in response. "I don't know," he mumbled. Mr. Balley, who heard snippets of the conversation from the front of the classroom, intervened as Dan began to walk away from the two girls.

"Mr. Verner, get back over here and tell me what you think you're doing." Ariana thought she saw Mr. Balley wink at her out of the corner of her eye and tried to suppress a laugh.

Dan, taken aback, slowly turned on his heels and approached Mr. Balley, who was advancing fast.

"I was just asking them to explain problem two on the homework to me, Mr. Balley."

"Really?" Mr. Balley said, placing his right hand pensively on his chin, "Because I heard something about how no one wants to have sex with me. Would you care to enlighten me as to how that came up in conversation?"

Ariana, suddenly emboldened by the smirks of the girl with the dreads, cut in. "Don't worry Mr. Balley, Val just said that to emphasize that you aren't having illicit relationships with any of your students."

"Ah, so you're the rumor mill, Mr. Verner." Dan gulped audibly.

"Well, I can confirm that myself and the other teachers in this building respect their students and their jobs too much to ever take advantage of anyone." He leaned in close to Dan and whispered something to him before resuming his teacher persona and walking back towards the front of the classroom. The rest of the class snickered.

"Okay, that's enough amusement for the day, let's get on with it," Mr. Balley said. Dan retreated to his seat, his saunter reduced to a sulk. Ariana was trying to focus on the lesson when the loud speaker asked that both of them report to the principal's office.

Ariana shot out of the door like a bullet while Dan hung back, walking as slowly as possible. Ariana was surprised to see Kelsey in the principal's office when she concluded her hallway sprint. She sat down next to her, breathless.

"What's going on?"

"I reported Dan's vandalism on your locker," she said.

"That wasn't Dan!" Ariana hissed. "It was Marcy. Trust me, I know. We vandalized the old fire tower together a few weeks ago and that's her handwriting."

Kelsey sucked her breath in and mouthed "oops".

"I'm sorry," she whispered.

"It's fine," Ariana said through gritted teeth. She moaned and sat back against her chair, banging her head against the wall in the process. *Great, now I have to sit down next to him and he's going to get pissed at me for getting him in trouble for the second time in one hour,* she thought through the haze of pain.

"That sounded like it hurt," Kelsey said softly.

"Yeah," Ariana said, rocking herself to an upright position and lightly touching the back of her head to ascertain that she wasn't bleeding. Dan walked through the door and the receptionist motioned for him to sit next to the girls. He sat down in the empty seat next to Ariana and glared at Kelsey. Kelsey caught his gaze and shrunk back into her chair. Dan pulled out his phone and began scrolling through Instagram. Ariana glanced at Kelsey, who shook her head in response. The three of them sat there in relative silence for about five minutes before the principal walked out of his office and collected Ariana and Dan. He was a stout man of about forty-five and had a brown mustache that reminded Ariana of a caterpillar. With an innocent round face and doe eyes, it was hard to take the man seriously. As they entered his office, he motioned for the two of them to sit side by side in the two chairs in front of his desk. He sat down and folded his hands together to address them.

"Thank you both for coming down here," he said, smiling at Ariana and grimacing at Dan. "It has come to my attention that an inappropriate word has been vandalized on Miss Demchuk's locker," he said, this time obviously looking at Dan. "We don't tolerate vandalism here. We especially don't tolerate it when it's used to put down other students. This constitutes bullying and is punishable by a week of in-school suspension."

"Mr. Wesley, I didn't do it," Dan protested, a

pleading look in his eyes.

"I didn't say you did," Mr. Wesley said, leaning back in his chair. "Miss Demchuk, do you believe that Mr. Verner was responsible for the vandalism on your locker?"

Ariana hesitated. *I mean, technically he's the one who has actively been making my life hell,* she thought.

"Indirectly," she answered. She could feel Dan's eyes boring down on her as if they were trying to rip her jugular out.

Mr. Wesley leaned forward in his chair and hunched over his desk.

"Care to elaborate?" He glared at Dan again before turning his full attention to Ariana. It was clear from the disgusted way he looked at Dan that he had been the quiet boy in high school that boys like Dan had picked on. She tried to conceal her smile as she began.

"Well, he started some rumors that might have inspired someone else to vandalize my locker."

"Ah," Mr. Wesley said. He leaned back into his chair again, as if contemplating what he had just heard. Once he was done thinking, he shifted forward again and hunched over his desk. He made eye contact with Dan and locked him in his gaze.

"Is this true, Mr. Verner?"

Dan looked immobilized to Ariana and she couldn't believe what she was seeing. The man who looked like he belonged in some light-hearted children's movie was absolutely terrifying to one of the biggest jocks she knew. She wished she could have that effect on someone.

Dan hesitated. "Y-Y-Yes," he said.

Satisfied, Mr. Wesley glanced up at Ariana with a small smile. "You can go now, Miss Demchuk. One of the janitors is cleaning up your locker as we speak."

Ariana stood up and walked out of the office. Kelsey was still there when she walked out. Ariana gave her a puzzled look and Kelsey got up and walked out with her.

"I wanted to make sure you were alright," Kelsey said, as they shut the door to the principal's office.

"Aside from the minor concussion I gave myself earlier, I guess I'm as good as I can be. It's good to know there's some sort of justice in the world. Dan's definitely never going to speak to me again now." She sighed and Kelsey echoed her.

"I think I'm gonna leave now," Ariana said, "too much excitement for one day."

Ariana packed up her things and made the long trek home again. This time, she couldn't stop thinking about the irony of skipping school. She used to use school as an escape from home, a place to be away from her father. Now she felt as trapped at school as she did at home. She wondered if that was the reason Teddy always hung out at Dexter's. She needed to find a safe haven of her own.

She considered going to the library, then decided against it because it was too quiet there and there was too much time to think. She considered going to Starbucks, but also concluded that it gave her too much time to think. She finally decided that she would have to frequent the mall more because it was loud, bright, and always busy. It reminded her of a microcosm of a city and she liked that. She longed for the anonymity of a city, of being able to be part of the crowd without standing out. She also liked people watching and wondering what her life would be like if she had been born in a different neighborhood in a different town. She wondered what life would be like if she had an artist for a father, or a carpenter. She wondered if he would teach her to paint and use power tools and if she would be the muse for all he did. Despite her wish for anonymity in the larger world, she longed to be the center of someone else's universe in her smaller world. She had thought she had been the center of Dan's universe, but he was quickly proving that was never the case.

She also thought that she used to be the center of Teddy's universe. She remembered him teaching her how to play soccer and how to blow up water balloons. She remembered him teaching her how to get out of a Chinese finger trap when she freaked out and got stuck in it. She also remembered that he was the one who had fooled her into putting her fingers in it in the first place (she had been seven at the time), but he got her out. *I suppose that's what brothers do*, she thought, *they torture you but then save you from their wrath.* She was about two tenths of a mile from home when she began crying uncontrollably for the brother she had lost somewhere in time. She hadn't realized that she missed him until that moment and regretted pushing him away recently.

When she finally arrived at her house, Teddy was in the living room. This time, he was surrounded by a cloud of smoke and Ariana was reminded that her brother had done some drifting away of his own.

"Do you want a hit?" he asked as she dropped her backpack by the door.

"Do you want Mom and Dad to murder you?" she said, walking towards him.

"That's child abuse," he said, fingering the joint in his right hand and examining it.

"No, that's homicide," she said, "which you would know if you weren't high."

"Relax, they're not home right now," Teddy said, taking another hit. He blew a ring of smoke out and leaned further back into the couch.

"You're fucked, you know that, right? How am I supposed to keep defending you to them when you do shit like this? I have enough problems of my own. This is the last thing I need."

"Don't count me as one of your problems," he said defensively.

"Fine," she said angrily. She turned around and walked out of the living room. Before she reached the kitchen, Teddy called out to her.

"What are you doing?"

She didn't bother stopping to respond.

"Going to my room," she yelled as she crossed through the kitchen and headed up the stairs.

Ariana slammed the door behind her. She was more fed up than she realized. She knew he would never understand what happened on Friday night. She couldn't tell him that the night he picked her up from Bryce's party was the same night she had drunkenly lost her virginity to her boyfriend's best friend. She couldn't tell him that Dan had broadcast the hook up to the whole school and that the popular people who had wanted to be her friends had disowned her. She couldn't tell him that the reason she had left school yesterday was because Dan refused to listen to her side of the story and Marcy had vandalized her locker. She didn't want to tell him that the reason she left today was because Dan and her had made an impromptu trip to the principal's office. She didn't want him to know that she only had one friend at the moment, and that even she wasn't entirely sure where Kelsey's loyalties lied. She wondered why Kelsey had even bothered to go to the principal's office in the first place. Ariana didn't see how that was supposed to help the situation.

When she retreated to her room, she sat down at her desk and grabbed the journal to her left. She opened it and began to read over what she had already written.

Thoughts Assembled

Sometimes I have so much to say that I end up saying nothing at all. I think that's what happens when you have a lot of secrets. Especially ones that aren't your own. There's so much pressure to keep up a façade that saying anything important feels like saying too much.

I wish I could erase it all. The pain, the memory, the guilt. I shouldn't have drank that much or even danced with Zach. I should have known better.

I can't believe Dan has the balls to call me an awful person when he started dating Marcy immediately after we broke up. You can't tell me that they all of a sudden developed feelings for each other. Maybe he's trying to make me look bad so that no one realizes that he's the real jerk. Don't get me wrong; I feel awful about the whole thing but what else can I say? I apologized profusely and I know that never would have happened if I wasn't so drunk. I just wish he could see that the girl who had sex with Zach was so not me.

She paused, unsure of how she felt about it. She

felt it was childish in a way, but at the same time putting a pen in her hand had felt so good. *Maybe today's thoughts will come out better,* she thought as she reached for a black fountain pen lying in front of her.

Things I want to say to Teddy

How does your ignorance supersede every other quality? Really Teddy, you can't keep doing shit like this. I'm sick of it. Mom and Dad are sick of it. Why can't you be the brother you used to be? I remember when you cared about things like school and soccer and hanging out with me. And don't say that you didn't care, because you were great at soccer and you loved math, and I'd ask you to help me if you would come down to planet earth every once in a while. Don't tell me Dad ruined your life because he ruined mine too, just in different ways. While he was off drilling you with soccer and school work, I was left alone, waiting for someone to come home and entertain me because Mom was too busy to when she was auditioning and physically couldn't after she got injured. And you never came home in time. I was always getting ready for bed and getting sweaty hugs and kisses from you guys right after you walked in the door. I'd go to bed smelling like BO and questioning the intention behind the hugs and kisses. They just felt like a routine you guys went through.

I guess it's a good thing I'm a dancer because I'm an

expert at pretending and dancing along with Dad. He feels guilty towards me, or at least obligated, so when he has his moments of weakness, I take advantage. You never did that, and still don't. Why do you think he always gives me money at family gatherings? He wants to make a show of it, to say, "Hey, look at what a good father I am." I pretend to be the ever gracious, but not spoiled daughter, who says, "But Dad, that's a lot of money," and then turns his insistence into a gift of $200.

I know that it's painful to play his game and I sometimes feel guilty, but it's necessary for survival. You can't keep fighting someone who always thinks they are right. You need to watch who he's around, who he's trying to impress, and figure out why he's acting the way he is. Then you need to play along with it for the sake of saving face because everyone else sees him as a charismatic lawyer, a breath of fresh air compared to most of the sticks in the mud that come out of law school. If we act out of resentment, then he gets his way: he looks good and we look like ungrateful children. If we play his game, he looks good and we don't look horrible. Have you picked up on the theme yet? He will ALWAYS win.

So if you really want to spite the man, stop smoking all the time and get on your feet. Get a job doing something you want to do and show him that money isn't the most important thing in the world. Haven't you heard the saying, "success is the best revenge"?

Satisfied that her aggravation was off her chest, she closed her journal, stood up and pushed her desk chair in. She curled up in the fetal position on her bed and fell asleep.

Teddy kept smoking downstairs while Ariana slept. He got into a rhythm where he would take a hit, wait ten minutes, then take another. He did this for another hour. He normally didn't smoke for that long but something about Ariana's reaction had upset him. He got the sense that he was letting her down. He had started avoiding his house to keep his father off his back, but he hadn't intended to isolate himself from the rest of his family in the process. Once the joint was almost gone, he put it out under the coffee table and then placed it on the table. He leaned back on the couch and pulled out the recliner. As he lay in his stupor, he tried to remember the last time he had spent time with Ariana and his mother. He remembered picking Ariana up from a party last Friday but they hadn't really talked much on the ride home because she had been crying hysterically. He wondered again what had happened at the party but didn't want to upset his sister more by asking, especially not when he was high.

Once he resolved to talk to Ariana when he was sober, his sluggish thoughts slowly shifted to his mother. He felt bad that the last time they had talked one-on-one was when he was high. As he sank deeper into his subconscious, he realized that he wasn't sober for most of the conversations he had recently. He was too stoned to act on any of his thoughts though, so he let himself be consumed by the smoke around him and fell asleep.

* * *

Frank came home from work at five and was assaulted by the smell as soon as he walked through the door. He saw Teddy sleeping on the couch and shook his head. He unbuttoned the top button on his shirt and loosened his tie before dropping his briefcase by the door and walking into the kitchen. He rummaged through the fridge, hoping there were still leftovers from the night before. Instead, he found a jar of sauerkraut, a half-eaten bag of baby carrots, a half-eaten container of hummus, and ground turkey. Unsatisfied with his search, he slammed the fridge and walked past the eat-in -kitchen to get to the pantry. Instead of finding the usual potato chips and Oreos, he found snap pea crisps, pistachios and chocolate covered almonds. Baffled by how quickly his house was beginning to look like a sparsely stocked Whole Foods, he settled on pistachios and almonds. He grabbed his snacks, sat down at the kitchen table, and stared at Teddy sleeping in the other room. He fought the urge to storm into the room and threaten to kick him out, knowing that if he kicked him out of the house in this instant, he would still have to come back and get his things. Frank wanted him and his attitude to be gone for good. He couldn't even imagine what his father would have done to him if he had been caught with weed. Frank shifted in his seat at the thought of being beaten.

He remembered how motivated his son was when he was thirteen and trying out for competitive travel teams. Frank loved getting on the field with Teddy and helping him practice. He had felt like he was reliving a youth he never had. The best moments they had were usually in their backyard when they were just kicking a ball around.

"You know, your mother wants me to talk to you about something," Frank had said one day as he passed the ball to Teddy.

"What?" Teddy asked, his voice rising in inflection at the end. He chased after the ball, turned quickly on his heels, and returned it.

"Well, she found a magazine in your room," Frank began, grimacing and holding the ball hostage. He couldn't blame his son for being curious but his wife had thrown a fit about those types of magazines objectifying women. Frank had never personally seen an issue with them and kept his own collection in the same small safe under their bed that he kept his hand gun in. He had a feeling that he had carelessly thrown one of them under the bed without locking the safe one night and that Teddy had found it during one of his games of hide and seek.

"Oh God, really?" Teddy rolled his eyes and put his head down in shame.

"Yeah," Frank said, "and she wants me to give you the talk." Frank lightly kicked the ball towards Teddy, making him run forward and sprint back after he tapped it back towards his father.

"Dad, I already know what you're gonna say. Can we not make this awkward and just say we talked about it?"

"I guess," Frank said, kicking the ball back to Teddy. "Just promise me that you'll always use a condom and be safe."

Nancy interrupted Frank's flashback when she walked through the door half an hour later. "Wow, it reeks in here," she said, walking over towards Frank at the table. She kissed him on the cheek and hung her gym bag up on the chair next to him.

"Geez, you reek too," he said, looking up at his sweaty wife. She was wearing a baggy light blue shirt that was turning dark blue from sweat. Her hair was pulled back into a ponytail and her face was still flushed.

"Since when do you go to the gym?" he asked.

She sauntered over to the kitchen and opened the

fridge. She grabbed carrots and hummus, shut the door, and sat down next to Frank, who was trying to decide what was more offensive: the smell of cheap marijuana or his wife's body odor. *Either way, the combination isn't great*, he thought.

"Since I'm trying to be healthy," said, crunching a carrot, "I told you this the other day. Oh and I got a personal trainer," she added, avoiding eye contact. She dipped a carrot into her hummus and crunched into it.

"Jesus Nancy, do you know how much that costs?" he yelled, his face becoming flushed.

She looked up and stared him right in the eyes. She wanted to scream back but replied back in a normal tone of voice.

"There's actually a two-week trial going on now where it's discounted. I think that once I get into the groove of doing it for a couple weeks, I won't need the trainer anymore. I just need to get into a routine."

"And how much is that gym membership going to be?" he asked. The nuts hadn't satiated him in the least and his hunger was worsening his already heated temper.

"$10 a month," she said, raising her voice slightly. She wanted to remain calm, but her husband always made it difficult.

"That's $10 that could be going towards Ariana's

education!" he yelled, slamming his hands down on the table and standing up. His chair squeaked as he practically threw it behind him.

Ariana, hearing her name, quietly opened the door of her room and tip toed halfway down the stairs to eavesdrop. Meanwhile, Frank's screaming had woken Teddy up and he began to slowly open his eyes. He was careful not to move much for fear his father's rage would turn towards him.

Nancy stood up in response. "Oh please, you bring home nine grand a month not including your investments. And you could send her to school by just selling stocks. Don't pull this money bullshit with me, Frank. I'm sick of hearing it. I don't work because I have to but because I want to. It's one of the only things that gives me a purpose in life anymore!" she said, throwing her hands up in the air for emphasis. "The kids don't need me and you're never home so what am I supposed to do? Sit on the couch eating bon-bons all day? Hell, I'm trying to lose weight."

"Oh, so that's why there's no food in the house," Frank yelled.

"Really? Do you have to make me feel like shit about everything? I used to love you but I don't know if you ever loved me. I think you just liked the idea of a little dancer that you could toss about in your bed and now that I'm old and fat you don't care."

"How can you say that?" Frank yelled. All the blood in his body rushed to his face and he felt his heart leap up to his throat.

Nancy caught a twinge of fear in her husband's eyes. "How dumb do you think I am? I know that you've been spending late nights at bars and I didn't want to say anything because I didn't have any proof, but now I do. Isabelle told me about you two the other day and I want a divorce."

Frank's face flushed redder than Nancy realized was possible, but for the first time in twenty some odd years, he was completely backed into a corner without an easy target to place the blame on. Ariana's breath caught in her throat as she realized the gravity of what her mother had just said.

"You're the one who drives me to drink! If you ever wanted to do something other than stay home and watch TV, maybe we'd be at the bar together."

Nancy felt like a knife was stabbing her in her chest, but she pushed through the pain.

"That's bullshit and you know it! I may have fallen for that in my twenties, but you're a grown man capable of making your own decisions. I'm not the reason you had an affair, you are. I'm done," she said, turning around and storming towards the stairs. Ariana turned around to run back up, but her mother was faster than she thought.

Nancy jumped when she almost ran into her daughter on the stairs. "Ari," Nancy said with a sigh.

"Yes?" Ariana said, swiveling her head around.

"How much of that did you hear?"

"Most of it," Ariana admitted. She softened her gaze and tears welled up in her eyes when she saw the panicked look on her mother's face.

"I'm sorry," Nancy said as she walked up to the second to last step where Ariana was. She brushed her arm to comfort her.

"No, Mom, I'm sorry," Ariana said. She wondered if her drunken night with Zach had made Dan feel the way her mom was feeling and her stomach began to turn uneasily. When they reached the top of the stairs, Ariana gave her mother a real hug, trying to make up for the guilt she was feeling. Nancy tried to hold back tears so her daughter wouldn't see her cry.

"Are you and Dad really going to get a divorce?" Ariana said quietly, suddenly hoping her own act of infidelity would never be brought to light. She didn't want to be like her father, but was suddenly wondering if she had become him last Friday night. After all, it sounded like there had been a similar sequence of events: she had gotten drunk, cheated on her boyfriend, and had blamed the alcohol instead of herself. How was she any better?

"I think so," Nancy replied. The thought of it was both relieving and terrifying to her. Nancy pulled away, walked down the hallway to her room, and shut the door. Ariana turned the opposite way and retreated back to her room.

Once Nancy reached her bed, she collapsed onto it in the fetal position and started crying softly. She didn't want her husband to know she was anything but angry, nor did she want Ariana to pity her. Tux jumped up on the bed with her and started rubbing against her. She gently pet him as she cried and he eventually settled down near her face and stared at her.

"Oh Tux, what am I going to do?" she asked the cat when she stopped crying enough to talk. He meowed in response and rubbed his face against hers, brushing away some of her tears with the top of his head. She smiled at this and let out a small laugh, but tears were still streaming down her face.

"You know what?" she said to the cat, "we're finally going to get out of this place."

* * *

Teddy was trying to think of escape routes himself. He knew he couldn't pretend to be asleep forever. He was trying to determine the best way to get to his keys, which were in his room upstairs, and then make it to his car, which was in the garage that was two flights down, without being seen. He immediately regretted smoking in the house when he had woken up and discovered that the smell hadn't dissipated. He had smoked in the house before, but not nearly as much, and he always opened all the windows and tied dryer sheets to fans to make the stench go away faster. He had only opened one window, which hadn't done much more than make the room slightly cooler.

He watched his dad roam the kitchen, trying to find something to eat. He kept going back and forth between the pantry and the fridge as if the food he was craving would magically appear there. Finally, Frank decided that he needed to order take out and walked past the pantry and down the adjacent hallway towards Nancy's craft room to grab the folder of menus they stored in one of her closets. Teddy jumped up from the couch and soundlessly bolted upstairs. Both Ariana and Nancy had shut their doors, so he slipped into his room unseen. He shut the door behind him and grabbed his keys from his bureau, glancing towards the window. He sat down on his bed, trying to figure out how he would get down two flights of stairs without running into his father. He knew that Frank would be calling for take-out at any given moment and might go looking for Teddy if he bothered to glance towards the living room. He jumped up off his bed and looked out his window again, eyeing his car in the driveway then assessing the distance between his window and the ground. It was straight drop out into the front yard and even if he made the jump alright, he would land right in front of the dining room windows where his father would probably be sitting and snacking on chocolate almonds.

Deciding against the dangerous and bold option, he left his room, shut the door behind him, and knocked lightly on Ariana's door.

Ariana, who was on her bed reading the most recent issue of Teen Vogue to distract herself, got up and opened the door.

"What do you want, Teddy?"

"How'd you know it was me?" Teddy asked, shocked.

"Who else knocks like that? Mom and Dad don't have anything to be secretive about." After the words left her mouth, she frowned slightly, remembering the conversation she had just overheard.

"I wouldn't be so sure about that," Teddy said. He looked around her room for a second, trying to look inconspicuous.

"Yeah, I heard," she said, "That was a stupid thing for me to say. What do you want?" Her brother used to stall all the time when they were younger and he was trying to ask her for a favor, so she knew this game.

"Can I use your window?"

Ariana grabbed him by the shirt, pulled him into her room, and shut the door.

"I told you not to smoke in the house."

"I know, I won't do it again. Can you please help me out though? Dad's gonna kill me. Like he might actually murder me this time."

She rolled her eyes and let go of his shirt. Teddy attempted to make a sad face, but with all his anxiety, Ariana perceived extreme fear and concern and gave in.

"Fine," she said. She opened her window, which overlooked the backyard. There was a small patch of roof about six feet down that housed a small sunroom that they never used. Teddy pushed out the screen and it fell to the roof of the sunroom.

"You better fix my screen," she said as he lifted one leg out of the window, then the other.

"I will," he said, as he dangled from her window. He was grateful that he was tall and simply had to lower himself down to stand on the roof. Ariana watched him walk carefully to the far-right corner of the roof and get on his stomach. He inched his way down on the roof so that his feet began to dangle off, and once he reached the edge, hugged the corner, trying to get a grip on the lattice. She watched him climb down and saw him falter towards the bottom. He jumped down frantically, taking a small chunk of lattice with him. It glowed white on the green grass and he pocketed it, hoping no one would notice. He gave his sister two thumbs up, mouthed "thank you", and ran to the driveway to retrieve his car.

He didn't have a destination in mind until he realized he was heading towards New Haven. He took the scenic route through West Haven, past men in hoodies walking on the streets and vans advertising legal services. He found himself stopped at a light and saw a homeless man holding a sign. His gray beard hadn't been shaved in years and Teddy quickly looked away as soon as he spotted him. Teddy's gaze had lingered long enough for him to have made eye contact though, and given that he was the only car stopped at the intersection, he quickly locked his doors as the homeless man approached his car and walked around to the driver's side. Teddy forced himself to look straight ahead, ignoring the man tapping on his window.

"Can you spare some change? Help a guy out?" The man paused. "I haven't eaten in three days," he said.

Teddy ignored the man, gripping the steering wheel tighter. He quickly determined that no one was coming and blew through the red light, leaving the man behind.

Terrified as he was that the man would have used some sort of force to break into his car, he wondered how he had gotten there to begin with. Now that he was far enough away from immediate danger, he thought about how being homeless and being a prostitute, or being homeless and a druggie, usually weren't mutually exclusive and realized that if his dad kicked him out, he just might turn into the latter. He wondered if he would find himself taking advantage of the law-abiding citizens who stopped at intersections just so he could smoke, or even just afford a sandwich. He shook away the thought as quickly as it came and mumbled, "I'd never be like that," but wondered if he was lying to himself.

He parked his car in a parking garage and walked over to Bar. He showed the hostess his driver's license and she led him to a booth where he ordered a beer and a small mashed potato pizza. The restaurant was filled with young people drinking and laughing and Teddy found himself wondering when he had last laughed. One girl had a particularly sonorous laugh and caught his eye. She had short, curly, dark hair with pale skin and wore glasses with blue frames. She was pretty, but was far from the stunning girls who he had looked at through the pages of Playboy. She seemed interesting though and he decided that he wouldn't mind getting to know her. As he lifted a second slice of pizza to his mouth, a blonde girl approached him.

"Hey, are you here alone?" she asked, sliding into the booth across from him.

"Ugh, yeah why?"

"Do you wanna come sit with us?" she asked, nodding towards the table the girl he had been staring at was sitting at. Three other girls were sitting at the table with her. He looked dumbfounded.

The girl leaned in and said, "My friend with the glasses thinks you're cute."

"Sure," he said. Unsure of what was happening, he picked up his tray of pizza while the blonde girl carried over his half full beer and set it down on the table next to the girl with the glasses. The girl with the glasses shot her friend a dirty look and blushed as Teddy sat down next to her.

"So I take it you guys collect misfit toys, huh?" he said, addressing the group.

There was an awkward silence as the girls all glanced around at each other, wondering who the misfit was supposed to be. A few seconds passed before the blonde broke the silence.

"Yeah, we're all misfits in our own ways."

"Oh, I didn't mean you guys! I was just making a joke, cause I was sitting all alone and you took me in, y'know?"

A few girls at the other end of the table snickered.

"Oh, I'm sorry, we must have misunderstood," the blonde replied, laughing lightly. Teddy suddenly felt unwanted, but tried to shake the feeling away.

"I'm sorry, let's forget I ever said that. My name

is Teddy. Who is everyone else?"

The girls all went around the table and told him their names. The girl with the glasses was named Angelica. She blushed when she looked at him and he felt himself getting a bit red too. The blonde started a conversation with the other girls, allowing Angelica and Teddy to talk.

"So Teddy, what brings you to Bar alone on a Thursday night?"

Teddy swallowed. "I was just kind of driving around the area and got hungry."

"Oh, well you picked a good place," she said, sipping her lemonade.

"Yeah, I used to come here all the time when I went to UNH."

"Oh really? When did you graduate?"

Teddy sighed and hung his head. "I didn't."

"Aww, I'm sorry. Well what are you doing now?"

Teddy looked up slightly but let his shaggy brown hair shield his face.

"I'm currently between jobs," he said. "I was in excavation for the past couple years but the company I was working for went out of business."

"That sucks," Angelica said, frowning. "What are you looking for?"

"You know, I don't really know," he said, looking her in the eyes for the first time. He discovered that her soft brown eyes reminded him of melted chocolate.

"Well, what do you like to do in your free time?"

Get high, Teddy thought to himself. He racked his brain, trying to think of socially acceptable hobbies that didn't involve smoking weed. "I used to play soccer competitively," he said, suddenly realizing that his life had ceased to exist beyond clouds of smoke.

"Oh, so do you still play for fun?"

"No, it's not really fun for me. Actually, I don't think it ever was. I think I just did it to make my Dad happy."

"Oh." she said, taken aback.

"So what do you do for fun? Like what makes you happy?" she asked.

"I don't know. I guess I've never been truly happy." He paused and gave her a sad smile.

14

When the Smoke Clears

Teddy didn't come home until seven in the morning. After he had wrapped up his rather short conversation with Angelica and they had exchanged phone numbers, he had driven to the University of New Haven, parked near the main campus and smacked his head on the steering wheel repeatedly. Why had such a simple conversation been so hard? He tried to think of the last time he had a serious conversation with someone, but couldn't. He'd been out of a job for two months now and hadn't made much of an effort to find something else even though he had told his mom and his sister that he would two weeks ago.

As he sat in the parking lot of what might have been his alma mater, he found himself wishing he had done things differently. He wished he had cared enough to make it through his first year of college. He thought about how he would probably have a reliable job lined up for after graduation and would have probably saved up enough money to move out by now. Now he knew that independence wasn't a want, but a need, and felt tears begin to moisten his cheeks at the thought of his dad kicking him out on the street. He wiped them away and smacked his head on the steering wheel again, this time hitting the horn in the process. The blare rang out through the empty parking lot, startling him and a few sleeping birds in a nearby tree. He stared at the school, which now appeared to be mocking him.

He had fallen asleep sometime around three in the morning and woke up three and a half hours later to faculty filling up the parking lot. He started up his car and began driving home.

When he got home around 7:30, both his parents had left for work and his sister was sitting at the table, mushing her cereal with her spoon.

"Hey," he said, dropping his keys in his jacket pocket. He sat down next to her at the table.

"Hi," she responded. She glanced up at him for a second, then refocused her attention on her cereal.

"Did the bus already come?"

"Yeah. How was your prison break?"

Teddy leaned back in his chair thoughtfully. "It was alright. Do you need a ride?"

"No. I'm not going to school," Ariana said, standing up and walking towards the kitchen sink. She dumped her mush down the garbage disposal, rinsed her spoon and bowl, and put them in the dishwasher.

"Are you sick?" Teddy asked. She seemed more distant than usual.

"No," Ariana said, staring at the residual cereal in the sink.

"Then why aren't you going?" Teddy asked.

"I don't want to," she said, turning around and sitting back down at the table. This time she sat down across from Teddy, a defiant look on her face.

"Why not?"

"Because I don't want to."

Teddy pursed his lips, unsure of what to say next. The memory of wallowing in regret was so recent that it was pretty much all he could think about.

"Don't do what I did," he said softly. "Mom and Dad can't handle another wash-out."

"I'm not a wash-out," she said.

"Then what's going on? It's not like you to skip school," Teddy said, lowering his voice.

"Why do you care?"

"Because you're my sister."

"Really? Since when do you care? You're too busy getting high to focus on anyone but yourself."

Teddy sat in stunned silence, feeling his heart pound out of his chest. His sister had never acted this way before. In fact, when they were little and he would jokingly torture her by threatening to throw her dolls out the window, she wouldn't protest, but instead break down into tears, as if the loss of her doll was inevitable. What had changed? Had he missed some obvious sign? What was going on in her life? He suddenly realized that he didn't know anything about her life anymore. He remembered that she had been dating Dan Verner but couldn't remember if they were still dating. Had they gotten into a fight? Broken up?

"How's Dan?" he asked, thinking out loud.

"We're not dating anymore," she replied bitterly.

"What happened?"

"He dumped me because he thinks I'm a slut."

"Why?"

"Long story."

"Well if you're not going to school, we have all day."

"I'm not talking about this right now," she said, getting up and walking away with a mixture of anger and guilt in her stomach. She walked upstairs to her room and practically threw herself on her bed. There was a part of her that was angry at Teddy for suddenly showing interest in her life but another part that was secretly flattered. She wondered if maybe her brother was coming back to her but that also reminded herself that he had been fairly absent for the past four years. She didn't trust his interest in her life to last much longer than a week, if it even lasted longer than twenty-four hours. She grabbed her phone off of her bedside table and went to her gallery. She clicked on her screenshots and re-read Marcy's post from the night before. A picture of her and Dan popped up on Ariana's screen and she cringed at the picture of Dan and Marcy sitting by Dan's fireplace.

Nothing like a nice relaxing night by the fire with your boo #cuddles #fall #pumpkin spice

Ariana remembered the gut punch she felt when she saw that post at eleven the night before. She had decided then and there that she was too distraught to go to school the next day. Her guilt had quickly shifted back to anger. How could he accuse her of cheating when he and Marcy had clearly had some sort of flirtation going on while they were dating? She had cried herself to sleep, hoping to find refuge in her dream world, but that too was infiltrated by Marcy and Dan. She had dreamed they were making out in front of her locker and parting ways only to reveal the black marker staring her down.

She had woken up angrier than the night before, which confirmed her previous decision not to go to school. She had a feeling that if she saw Dan or Marcy, she wouldn't be able to resist confronting them and punching them and the last thing she needed was another trip to the principal's office. She hadn't known where this newfound aggression came from either. She assumed that it was probably because she saw Dan as an insufferable hypocrite for dating Marcy within a week of their break up. How come she was the slut but he was completely innocent? And did the fact that she was angry even though she had cheated and escalated the situation make her just as bad as her dad? As she sat on her bed and contemplated her new attitude, she suddenly realized that Dan's brazen accusation in math was what had triggered her sadness to turn into anger. That was when she realized that she could flip the script by not reacting to him. She suddenly realized that skipping school was a reaction too, and one that gave him power over her. She silently resolved to use the day as a means of catching up on her schoolwork so that she wouldn't risk ruining her future because of him.

As she sat down at her desk to start doing her homework, the memory of the pregnancy test that she had bought with Kelsey suddenly seeped into her mind. Her period was only three days late, but the thought of being pregnant was so terrifying that she dropped her pencil and reached under her bed to retrieve the test. She glanced over the box and took it into the bathroom with her. She opened it and carefully read the instructions, her heart beginning to race. She tried to remind herself that even if she was pregnant, she would figure something out.

Once she had read through the instructions twice, she took the dipstick out and removed the cover, staring at the blank space where a plus or minus sign would decide her fate in just a few minutes. She followed the instructions and set the dipstick down on a tissue on the bathroom counter. She washed her hands quickly, then pulled her phone out of her pocket and Googled "chemical abortions" while she waited for the test to determine her results. *This might actually be worse than taking a math test*, she thought as she read through the symptoms one experiences after taking the abortion pill. By the time she looked up from her phone, five minutes had passed and a blue minus sign had revealed itself. She breathed a sigh of relief, and began cleaning up after herself. She mummified the test in toilet paper and buried it in the trash can. Her face screwed up as she looked at the box, and she decided to slip it back under her bed until she could figure out a better way to discreetly dispose of it.

Ariana sat down at her desk again and was about to attempt her homework for the second time when she saw a Facebook message from Zach pop up on her screen. As much as she had emphasized Zach's role in Friday night's affair to Dan, she wasn't angry with him. She opened his message with curiosity.

Hey, how are you holding up?

Alright, I guess. You?

Well I'm not the one who's locker got vandalized. No offense or anything, but I didn't mean to sleep with you the other night. I never wanted to be that person to ruin a relationship like that, so I'm sorry.

Ariana sighed. *It's okay,* she said. *I think we were going to break up soon anyway.*

If it makes you feel any better, I'd be down to grab a consolatory cup of coffee. I know you have it way worse than me and I feel bad because it's all my fault. Ariana smiled to herself. She had been blaming herself and Dan so much lately that it felt good to hear someone else feel awful about themselves.

No, it was my fault too, she typed back. *But I do think coffee might cheer me up. Sunday morning?*

Works for me.

As she was now officially distracted by the thought of getting coffee with Zach, Ariana spent some time journaling her thoughts and then creating a to-do list.

Teddy took a nap and woke up with a new purpose. He was still embarrassed that he hadn't even been able to carry on a normal conversation and, realizing how bleak his life was, he resolved to spend the rest of his day going on the dual search of finding a job and an apartment. He didn't have a lot of money saved, but he could afford two month's rent if he knew he had a job that would provide money for the rest. He was just beginning to clean up his resume when Ariana came downstairs to make herself some lunch. Teddy glanced up from his screen to see her rummaging through the fridge but didn't say anything. She pulled out bread, hummus, bean sprouts, tomato, and spinach and made a sandwich. She ate standing up at the counter, not wanting to sit down and engage in conversation. Teddy continued making changes to his resume, adding in his recent excavation experience and changing some of the wording he had previously used. Ariana had heard the comedy show he had on for background noise as she walked downstairs and had assumed her brother was just watching TV. When she went back to the fridge to put the sandwich ingredients away, she noticed that he had a laptop on his lap. He seemed oddly focused and her curiosity broke the silence.

"What are you doing?"

"Working on my resume," he responded, only half looking up at her.

"Really?" Ariana said, coming closer. Part of her wanted to look at the screen for proof but another part was scared she'd find porn instead.

"Yeah. I can't sit around and smoke forever," he said, this time looking her straight in the eyes. His eyes were changed, wearied by the social and physical fatigue of the night before, yet no longer bloodshot. There was a hint of tired sincerity in them and Ariana thought she saw a glimpse of her old brother.

"Wow, I never thought I'd hear you say that," she said, sitting down on the couch next to him. "Do you want some help?"

As the hours of helping Teddy and reminiscing went on, Ariana found herself finding peace. It wasn't peace in the traditional sense, but she found herself realizing that she was giving the past too much power over her. As she was telling Teddy about the colleges and universities she was applying to, she found herself realizing that none of what had happened in the past week would matter in college. She found herself wondering out loud about what her roommates would be like, what college psych classes would be like, and what she should wear to class.

"Don't stress about it," Teddy said. "I think if I had taken college seriously, I probably would've done well. Just don't get behind and you'll be fine." He paused, cringing at his own failed experience.

"Just ask enough questions and you'll never be behind," he added. He wished he had been able to swallow his pride and ask for help instead of being arrogant and hoping the answers would come to him when he was high.

"You're smarter than me though, so you'll do

fine," he said.

"You're smart too," Ariana said. "You got great grades when you tried. You just need to apply yourself."

"Pun intended," Teddy smiled, as he hit the "Apply" button on an excavation job.

Both Ariana and Teddy were hard at work when their mother and father came home at 6 and 6:30, respectively. They had moved to the kitchen table so that Ariana had room to spread out her math homework. Teddy was looking into prices of apartments in the area and helping Ariana whenever she got stuck. Nancy was happily shocked when she walked through the door and witnessed the two of them helping each other. A rush of satisfaction washed over her sweaty body. She dropped her gym bag by the door and asked them what they were doing. Her mouth dropped open when Teddy told her he was looking for an apartment.

"You know how expensive that is, right?" she said, hovering over his screen to look at the lowest going prices.

"Yeah, but once I have a job, I'll be fine," he said.

"Have you been looking for jobs?" she asked.

"Yeah I just started."

"He applied to five companies today," Ariana cut in, sensing her mom's disbelief.

"Wow, that's great!" Nancy said. "Hopefully you

get at least one interview out of that."

"Yeah, hopefully," he said. "I'm sorry about last night by the way."

"Oh Teddy, don't worry about it," Nancy said, reminded not of the fact that the house had reeked of weed but of the fight she had with her husband.

"Are you sure?" He cast Ariana a sideways glance and she shrugged her shoulders.

"Yes, I'm positive. Your father and I are going to talk about it tonight."

"Okay," he said warily.

Nancy walked into the kitchen and tried to distract herself by fixing dinner. She pulled a fillet of salmon out of the fridge and cut it up. She then bent down, grabbed a skillet out of the cabinet, and placed it on the stove. She reached over to the right of the stove to grab a bottle of olive oil and swirled it around the pan before putting in the fillet. She then grabbed some green beans, put on a pot of water and steamed them while the salmon sizzled.

Frank walked through the door right as Nancy was flipping the salmon over. Ariana glanced up from her homework and Teddy flinched, fighting the urge to run away. He knew his father wanted to murder him for smoking in the house yesterday and was terrified.

"Teddy, what are you doing home?" Frank asked. He had hoped that Teddy might have moved himself out in anticipation of his rage.

"I'm looking for jobs," Teddy replied, his eyes glued to his laptop.

"Really? Has the smoke finally cleared? Cause it sure as hell wasn't cleared out of here last night."

Teddy winced and didn't acknowledge his father, who was the reason he had started smoking to begin with. He vividly remembered his dad saying, "If I survived law school, you can survive high school," when he finally cracked under the pressure of taking all advanced courses in his sophomore year of high school.

"But Dad, you didn't have to take classes this hard when you were my age."

"Don't make excuses for yourself," his father had responded before retreating into his study.

Teddy was tired of repeating that situation over and over again. He didn't want his father to talk to him because it was never a conversation; it always turned into a lecture. Teddy realized that this wasn't discriminatory to him specifically, as he had seen his father lecture both sister his and his mother, but it still irked him, especially when his father launched into a diatribe about how he wasn't nearly as hard on Teddy and Ariana as their grandfather was on him.

Frank, unsatisfied with the lack of reaction he roused from Teddy, turned towards his wife. He set his briefcase down on the countertop and asked Nancy how her day was.

"Okay," she responded, keeping her back to him as she cooked. She half-heartedly asked him how his day was and he launched into a story about how one of his clients had broken his soon to be ex-wife's restraining order against him and tried to pick their daughter up from daycare. Nancy shot Ariana a tired glance and motioned for her to set the table. Ariana got up to grab plates and interrupted Frank's story.

"Wait, is this the drug addict? You know, the one who snorted coke in front of his kid?" Ariana cut in.

"Yeah," Frank sighed.

"Geez Dad, why do you represent the scum of the earth? He was probably trying to kidnap his daughter in some drug-induced haze," Ariana said, setting down the plates and silverware on the table. She gave one set of everything to Teddy, who pushed it aside, and then proceeded to set the other places.

"Nah, I think he just wanted to see her. He's seen her maybe twice in the past year."

Lucky, Teddy thought to himself, *if only I could see my Dad twice a year.* He found himself wishing that his mother had married someone different because then he might not even exist. He began contemplating the thought of never being born when his mother yelled that dinner was ready. He grudgingly shut his laptop and moved it to the coffee table in the living room. He then grabbed his plate and walked over to the counter to serve himself. They served themselves in silence, Ariana brooding over her dad's defense of horrible people, Frank annoyed at his daughter for questioning him, Nancy trying to hide how much she wanted to run out of the house and never look back, and Teddy trying to maintain a semi-poised composure for the confrontation that both he and Frank knew was about to come.

They all served themselves quickly, sat down at the table, and began eating. With the exception of a couple compliments to Nancy for making dinner, silence permeated the room. Finally, Nancy spoke up.

"How was everyone's day?" she asked, directing the question towards her children. Teddy and Ariana hesitantly looked up from their food.

"Productive," Ariana said, making eye contact with her mother for a second before looking back down at her plate.

"Well that's good," Nancy began, "but strange, because I got a call from school saying you weren't there today."

Ariana's heart started beating faster and she could feel her face turning red.

"I needed a mental health day," she said. "I was getting really behind in math, so I took today off to get some rest and get caught up. I'm almost done now," she said, impressed with her lie. She even managed to convince herself that she had intended to skip school for noble reasons.

Nancy, who knew that her daughter had been struggling in math and saw the pleading look in her eyes, believed her.

"Oh honey, you should have just said something. I could have called you out sick."

"I didn't want to bother you," Ariana said. She couldn't believe that she hadn't thought of lying to her mom in advance and silently cursed to herself.

"So what about the lecture you missed today?" Frank cut in, "Doesn't that just make you fall further behind?"

"Dad, I needed a day off to catch up. What I missed in one lecture is a lot less to make up than all the homework I fell behind on."

"Well, why did you fall behind in the first place?"

Ariana looked down at her plate and hesitated. "Because math is hard, okay?"

"You know what's hard?" Frank said, "Law school. And being an adult."

"Dad, shut the fuck up!" Teddy yelled. He stood up, practically throwing his chair out from underneath him in the process and causing it to squeak across the floor. "You think that you're the smartest and greatest person in the world because you made it through law school, but guess what, you're not! You used to pull this shit with me all the time and I'm sick of it. You don't respect anyone else's lives because it's not the way you live. Not everyone wants to go to court for druggies who try to kidnap their children. I'm so sick of you pressuring us to be something we're not." Teddy turned around and walked towards the stairs, his face beet red. He could feel angry tears forming in the corner of his eyes but waited until he rounded the corner to wipe them.

Frank, who had stood up in the heat of Teddy's monologue to counter him, slowly lowered himself back into his seat as he watched his opportunity to kick his son out retreat. His instinct was to yell up the stairs, "Then move out of the fucking house!" but the thought of kicking him out no longer seemed as satisfying at it had the previous night, so Frank remained seated and silent.

"So," Nancy cut in, trying to redirect the conversation, "you had a mental health day." Ariana nodded in response.

"Frank, how was your day?" Nancy asked.

"Alright. I visited Dad at lunch," he said, shoveling food into his mouth.

"How's he doing?" Nancy asked, feigning interest. She wasn't entirely sure if she believed the horror stories her husband had told her about the way his father treated him when he was growing up and but there was a part of her that wondered if his father's condition was some sort of karmic retribution.

"Eh, not so great. He keeps falling, so he's pretty

bruised."

"Poor Grandpa," Ariana cut in. She no longer felt any sympathy for her father, the one witnessing his decline.

"Yeah, you and Teddy should get down there and see him soon. I don't think he has much longer," Frank said with a sigh. The thought of his father made him want to vomit all of a sudden and he stopped eating.

"I'm not super hungry right now," he said. "I think I'm going to go upstairs and lie down." He stood up and carried his plate and silverware over to the sink. He then walked past his wife and daughter to go upstairs.

Once he reached the master bedroom, he flopped down on the bed. He lay on his back and stared up at the ceiling fan. He was conflicted: he and his dad hadn't exactly had the best relationship, but at the same time the man was dying. When he had to rush to the nursing home at lunch time after getting a call that his dad had a bad fall and might need to go to the hospital, Frank hadn't been able to rouse sympathy for the man who had whipped him when he had misbehaved and gotten bad grades. As the only son and their first child born in the United States, he was the one who was supposed to help his family build the American dream. His father had received a degree in Ukraine in the 1950's, but that degree had meant next to nothing in the United States job market. He had ended up working in a manufacturing plant and wanted his son to pursue law or medicine so that he would be guaranteed financial security.

Frank remembered being about nine years old when he received his first C in science. His father had whipped him with his belt, each thud reverberating in Frank's skull. Frank had never done that to his children and wondered if maybe he should have.

In a room at the other end of the hall, Teddy was still fuming. He imagined smoke coming out of his ears and nose and liked the image it conjured. He felt like a riled bull, ready to attack anything that dared to move in the wrong direction. He was high off of the adrenaline of truly standing up to his dad for the first time in his life. Teddy was still shocked that Frank hadn't shouted gibberish at him as he had ascended the stairs.

Nancy and Ariana were still slowly eating a silent dinner. They occasionally made eye contact and glanced upstairs, as if they were both expecting the upper level of their house to spontaneously combust. They barely made any noise, even as they both started cleaning the kitchen. Nancy nodded to Ariana to load the dishwasher while she wiped down the counter. Ariana nodded back and began rinsing dishes off quietly. She gingerly placed each dish in the dishwasher so as to not make any noise.

She felt that her mother's silence was due in part to Teddy's outburst, but after the previous night, knew there was probably more to it. Ariana embraced the silence as a way to see a more vulnerable side of her mother. Somehow she had forgotten that her mom had feelings like everybody else and felt a strange intimacy in the silence.

As Ariana was contemplating the silence, Nancy wasn't even aware of it; her mind was buzzing with thoughts that seemed quite loud to her.

This is proof that you need a divorce, she thought. *Who wants to live in a house like this?* She finished wiping down the counter and then moved to the gas stove. She gently lifted the grill of each burner off and set it next to its respective burner on each side of the counter. She sprayed the stove and began wiping it down in a circular motion.

What if he doesn't want a divorce and tries to fight me on it? I can't afford to hire a lawyer to fight for me in court. Oh God, I don't know if I can do this.

But he has been spending a lot of time at the bars and he did cheat on me, so that should be enough to justify a decent alimony payment if I take the chance on hiring a lawyer.

Oh, maybe I should wait until after Christmas. Don't want to ruin the holidays.

"Mom," Ariana interrupted, "I think that burner is clean." Ariana had finished the dishes and was leaning against the counter. She had been watching her mom compulsively scrub the same area over and over again for the past five minutes.

Nancy looked down at the spotless burner. "Oh yeah," she said, and moved on to the one behind it.

"Are you okay?" Ariana asked.

No, Nancy wanted to say. *I'm trying to start living again but I still feel stuck.*

Instead, she said, "Yeah, just a little preoccupied, that's all." She paused as she switched gears and started cleaning the burner to the right. "Did you start your Christmas shopping yet?"

"I got Kelsey something but I'm not sure about Dad and Teddy. I figured we'd buy something for them together."

"Yeah, we can go to the mall on Friday." Nancy looked down at the burner she was cleaning and started scrubbing at some dried food.

"What about Dan?" Nancy asked.

Ariana looked down at her feet. The mention of his name still had the power to bring tears to her eyes, not because she missed him, but because she missed the idea of him. She was also still feeling a little guilty about Zach and didn't want to tell her mother what had happened for fear that she would look like her dad. She wondered if her mother would ever be able to forgive her for what she had done if she knew and a tear escaped. She quickly wiped it away, took a deep breath and swallowed her tears back before telling her mom they had broken up.

"Oh honey, I'm so sorry," her mom said, dropping her rag on the stove and hugging Ariana.

"It's okay," Ariana said, sniffling back tears, "I'm better off without him anyway."

"Well that's a good attitude," Nancy said, releasing her hug and standing back to look at her daughter. Her face looked sad but her straight posture made her seem strong and resilient. Nancy admired this and resolved to stop putting off her request for a divorce. She no longer cared about ruining Thanksgiving or Christmas for him; she was concerned about giving herself a good new year.

15

The Divorce

The next morning, Nancy dressed for work and walked downstairs to confront Frank, who was still in his pajamas. Between his messy hair and the bags under his eyes, Nancy could tell he had a rough night on the couch. He was sitting at the kitchen table, nursing a cup of coffee. She pulled out a chair and sat down across from him.

"Listen, we need to talk," she said.

"I don't want to talk," he said, rubbing his eyes.

"Well I meant what I said the other night," she said.

"Fine, what do you me to do right now? I may be an attorney but I can't divorce us overnight."

Nancy tried to hide the shock on her face, but her husband seemed so different all of a sudden. His eyes seemed dim, not penetrating like they normally were, and his angular face seemed softer in the early morning light that seeped in through the kitchen window. She couldn't place the emotion on his face, but if she didn't know any better, it was sadness. She wasn't sure if it was a ploy to evoke her sympathy though, so she avoided the subject.

"I'd like you to move out," she said, her lip trembling slightly.

"Okay," he said. He mumbled something about going to sleep at Andy's house for a few nights and then stood up and walked upstairs

Even though she was getting what she wanted, she was confused. She wasn't sure if she should be glad for his demure reaction or wary of it. She found his uncharacteristically calm behavior as unsettling as a tornado warning.

* * *

As Nancy was wrapping up her workout later that day, Ariana was trying to scrape together something to eat for dinner. She couldn't stop thinking about how Bryce was having another party tonight and how everyone was probably wondering if she'd have the audacity to show up. She opened the pantry, her eyes scanning the shelves for cookies or graham crackers to fill the hollow feeling in her chest but couldn't find any comfort food that was compliant with her mother's new diet. She found cheese and bread and began nibbling on the cheese. As she glanced over at the bread, she decided to make a grilled cheese and grabbed the butter out of the fridge. She buttered the bread, careful not to break it, and began assembling her grilled cheese in the pan that was already on the stove. Once she put the second piece of bread on, she pulled her phone out of her jeans pocket and checked her texts. She opened her conversation with Kelsey, who had sent her two texts.

You going to Bryce's tonight?
David and I can pick you up.

Ariana sighed and put her phone down on the counter. She grabbed a spatula out of a drawer and flipped her grilled cheese, revealing a golden-brown crust. She grabbed her phone again and looked hard at the texts. She didn't want to go to Bryce's party, much less third wheel with Kelsey and her boyfriend. She texted back that she couldn't go because she needed to help her mother with something even though Kelsey would see right through her flimsy excuse. She should understand why Ariana didn't want to go to another one of Bryce's parties. Ariana suddenly realized she was mad that Kelsey was going.

What if they turn her against me? Ariana thought as she lifted her grilled cheese to reveal a golden-brown crust forming on the other side. She shut the stove off and grabbed a plate and a knife. She cut her sandwich in half diagonally and took a bite, waiting for Kelsey to beg that she go to Bryce's party. The text didn't come though, and as Ariana finished her sandwich, she wondered if Kelsey was really on her side. She closed out her texts and went to Facebook where she searched on Kelsey's page, looking for a clue as to if she was a foe masquerading as a friend despite the fact that they'd been best friends for seven years. All she saw were posts of Kelsey's dog and boyfriend, along with the occasional food video. Satisfied but still suspicious, she closed out of Facebook and checked her texts. She saw a new text and tapped it to discover that it was Teddy.

Hey, is Dad home? he asked.

Not yet, she responded. She put her phone down and glanced at the kitchen clock to see that it was 6:45. Realizing how late it was, she picked her phone up again and texted back, *Maybe he went to the bar.*

Ariana left the pan on the stove to cool and rinsed her dishes off before placing them in the dishwasher. She then walked upstairs, grabbed a magazine from her bedside table, and plopped down on her bed.

Teddy came home roughly twenty minutes later. He yelled for Ariana, but she didn't hear him. He took his coat off and draped it over one of the chairs in the dining room. He walked upstairs and yelled her name again.

"What?" she yelled back, dropping her magazine

on the bed.

"What are you doing tonight?" he asked, out of breath from having run up the stairs. He stood in her doorway, looking anxious.

"Why do you care?"

"Because I need to do something. What do normal people do?"

"I don't know, go to the movies?"

"People do that sober?"

Ariana flipped herself over and sat up straight. She raised an eyebrow. "People do a lot of things sober. Like drive."

"What's wrong with you?" Teddy said, coming closer to his sister. He thought he saw a tear in the corner of her eye.

"Nothing," she said. Teddy raised his eyebrows back at her. She rolled her eyes, trying to suppress her tears.

"Fine, there's a party I've basically been uninvited to happening tonight. I don't want to go but Kelsey wants me to."

"I thought you said you were uninvited?"

"It's complicated. I don't think Kelsey is the person I thought she was. I guess no one is who I thought they were." She let some of her sobs go and Teddy ran over to her and hugged her.

"You can trust me," he said, "I'm gonna try to be a better brother."

"I don't know who I am anymore," Ariana said, crying onto Teddy's shirt. She wanted to tell him everything, how she had lost her virginity to a relative stranger and how she was secretly terrified of becoming her father but she was scared that if he saw a glimpse of their father in her, he would run away.

"It's okay," Teddy said, rubbing her back. "Sometimes you need to recreate yourself. I found a quote I really liked the other day: sometimes the old you isn't someone worth finding." He paused and considered the weight of his own words. "Why don't we try to find something fun to do tonight? Just the two of us."

One hour later, Ariana put on jeans and a light sweater and got in the car with Teddy. Their mother gave them a strange look as they left, but didn't say anything. She hadn't seen her children spend time together outside of the house since Teddy got his license. She wasn't sure if she should be concerned but decided that her kids probably weren't doing anything too crazy and continued watching Law and Order.

As Ariana and Teddy drove to the movie theater, they were careful to only make small talk. Both were too scared of offending the other in their fragile states. They tried to keep the focus of their conversations on their parents. They both marveled at the fact that their mom was trying to get in shape for the first time since she had injured herself. Ariana commented that she seemed happier and Teddy noted that she already looked like she was slimming down a bit even though it had only been about a week. After they came to the consensus that they were both proud of their mom, Teddy started talking about their dad and Ariana stiffened. She was angry at her dad for her own reasons but couldn't blame him for being mad at Teddy for wasting his time and becoming a pothead.

Oh my God, maybe I am becoming my father, she thought to herself. She quickly banished the thought and listened to his rant in silence until they got to the movie theater.

* * *

In a different car in a different town, Frank found himself parked in a Walmart parking lot. He knew that Andy wasn't a good enough friend for him to call in a favor for a sleepover and he hadn't talked to most of the contacts in his phone in ages. He considered calling his sister, but remembered that they hadn't talked about anything but his father's care in the past five years and decided against it.

He also could have gotten a hotel, but he didn't want to. There was a part of him that thought that maybe he could make things right if he paid his penance by living out of his car for a week.

As he sat in his car alone, he was reminded of the oppressive silence that had shrouded the house when he had returned at lunchtime to gather some things he had left behind in the morning. Despite the weight of everything, he lingered a bit and found himself standing in the middle of the living room, trying to ignore the tightening sensation in his chest.

Will I get the house in the divorce? he wondered. *Will this be one of the last times I step foot in it?* He had moved towards a window that faced the backyard and glanced out at the old goal posts he had set up from Teddy's soccer days. He remembered when his son liked him and they used to play soccer all the time. Frank wanted to know what had changed, and when. When had he become the opposing teammate instead of the coach? He hadn't dwelled on the thought too long though, as he didn't want to risk one of his family members making an impromptu trip home during the day.

When he realized that he was thinking too much, he put his car into drive and found himself pulling into the same dive he had run into Isabelle at the previous week. He fingered the wedding band he had taken off the week before and wondered what was next. Where would he go for Thanksgiving next Thursday? He and his sister weren't exactly on speaking terms and his mother was dead. He thought about visiting his dad, but immediately dismissed the idea in favor of drinking. He dropped his wedding band in his center console, shut it, and got out of his car.

Once he settled in at the bar, he ordered a scotch and watched the people around him having fun. It was an older crowd tonight but it was far from quiet. A group of three fifty-something men were loudly reminiscing about college together a few stools down from them and Frank began to wonder where he had went wrong. Where were his friends? He grabbed his phone from his pocket and was about to text Andy when he thought better of it. He didn't want aimless talk about football or girls. He wanted someone to help him, to tell him how to get his old life back. He ordered another scotch and started watching the bartender as he served everyone. He moved fluidly and smiled at everyone he was serving, even the 40-year-old women who were dressed like they were in their early twenties. Frank used to think he had a similar grace but now he wasn't so sure.

"Are you happy doing this, man?" Frank asked when the bartender offered a refill.

"I guess, yeah," the bartender replied, turning around to grab the scotch from the top shelf. He refilled Frank's glass and Frank took a small sip as the bartender returned the scotch to the shelf.

Frank pulled out his phone and checked his texts. Nothing. He didn't know what he was expecting. He put his phone back in his pocket and took a long sip of scotch. He put his glass down but the thought that he would have probably have to spend Thanksgiving at his dad's nursing home made him pick his glass back up and finish off his scotch in one long swig.

"You good?" the bartender asked, grabbing his glass for a refill.

"No," Frank said.

16

Death and a Motel 8

By the time Sunday morning rolled around, Frank had decided that Nancy wasn't going to call begging him to come home, so he finally got a motel room. After he had unloaded his car (which had been stuffed to the brim), he took a deep breath and lay down on the bed. He stared up at the dim ceiling light, glad that it wasn't bright. He normally didn't get hangovers, but the combination of scotch, stress, and sleeping in his car had accumulated into a throbbing sensation in his left temple. Suddenly, his phone rang, the tone tearing through his skull. He quickly grabbed his phone from the bedside table and answered it.

"Hello?" he said.

"Hi, Mr. Demchuk?"

"Yes,"

"This is Angie from Angel's Home Care. I'm calling

regarding your father, Yosyp Demchuk. He's had a pretty serious fall and will need to be transported to the hospital. I was trying to get a hold of your sister but I couldn't reach her. Your hospital of choice is Yale New Haven Hospital, correct?"

"Yes, I'll be down there in half an hour."

Frank put his phone in his pocket and flew down the highway, cursing himself out for getting a cheap motel room that was far away from everything. He could have afforded a nicer place, but wondered if maybe he could induce good karma if he made himself suffer. He promised himself that he would look for a more permanent place tomorrow morning and began imagining what his new place would look like.

It was much easier to think about his living situation than to focus on the pit in his stomach that told him that his father was dying. He knew he should be feeling remorse, but he couldn't help feeling relieved as he pulled into Yale's parking lot. He hurriedly got out of the car and practically ran to the reception desk like the concerned son he thought he should be. The receptionist directed him to his father's room and he ran to the elevator. By the time he reached his father's third floor room, it was loaded with doctors and nurses.

"What's going on?" he yelled, blocked out by a sea of white coats.

One of the attending doctors shouted some orders to his staff and walked towards Frank. He motioned for Frank to step outside the room and walked him to the third floor waiting room.

"I want you to know that we're going to do the best we can," the doctor said, "but it doesn't look good. Your father sustained a pretty serious fall for someone on a blood thinner."

"What? He fell just the other week and was fine."

The doctor sighed and put a hand on Frank's shoulder. Frank brushed it away.

"My file says he's been on Coumadin since a clot was discovered in his leg last week. He's severely bruised and we're going to do our best to control his bleeding but there's a risk that the clotting medication we have to administer to stop the bleeding will cause his current clot to worsen. There's a pretty high risk of stroke."

Frank's face flushed red with anger and he clenched and unclenched his fists to prevent himself from letting loose and punching a wall.

"So what happens if you don't administer the clotting medication?"

The doctor sighed heavily.

"Your father sustained a large gash on his head and his right arm when he fell. With the amount of blood he's already lost, he'd bleed out. If we administer Andexxa, which will stop the bleeding, we can safely give him a transfusion."

Frank stared at the doctor blankly, his red face paling to a light pink.

"I'm sorry," the doctor said, "we're going to try to do everything we can but your father is in a very precarious position right now." He patted Frank on the shoulder again and walked away to help his other patients.

Frank glanced around at the other people waiting teary-eyed and anxious and decided to channel his mixed emotions into pacing, which seemed like a more socially acceptable reaction. He paced for about thirty minutes, thinking about what would happen if his father died. He couldn't help but feel a sense of relief that all his depressing Sunday visits to the nursing home would be over.

When he got tired of pacing and decided to finally sit down, his sister walked in, her blond hair tied into a high bun and her face splotchy with tears. He immediately stood back up and felt his anger rush back to his face.

"Are you fucking kidding me, Lisa?" he yelled before she could even say hello. The entire waiting room fell silent and looked towards the two of them.

"You put him back on Coumadin after he has a fall? What were you thinking?"

"Well hello to you too," she said, wiping away tears. She took a moment to compose herself before speaking.

"If you must know, he was complaining about leg pain after the fall, so the nurses did some imaging and found a clot. Deep vein thrombosis. They said it looked large enough to cause an issue at any moment and told me that it was safer to put him on the blood thinner than to leave the clot as it was."

"So you gambled with his life?"

"It was a calculated risk," she said, sobbing, "He doesn't exactly have the highest quality of life anyway."

Her tears incited him to push her even farther over the edge than she already was.

Frank leaned towards her and lowered his voice so only she could hear him, "You know, if he dies, it'll be your fault. If he was still living at home with a caregiver who actually watched over him, this wouldn't have happened."

"He's not going to die!" she said before collapsing into a chair next to an older woman and her granddaughter. The older woman wrapped an arm around her and whispered something comforting in her ear. Frank started pacing again.

* * *

Ariana had a more pleasant wake-up call when she

walked into Starbucks and found Zach waiting for her at the counter, his hands in his pockets. The aroma of coffee and pastries wafted towards her, inviting her to approach Zach. He was about six feet tall and fairly muscular. When he turned to face her and met her gaze, she realized that he not only looked more attractive than Dan, but also seemed kinder.

"Hey, what do you want?"

"I'll take a medium latte," she said, suddenly wondering if this was less so commiserating over coffee and more so a date. They had slept together though, so maybe a date was in order, if not for romantic purposes, then at least to clear the air. Zach paid for her coffee and they sat down at a table once they got their drinks.

"You didn't have to pay back there," she said, "but thanks."

"No worries. I think you more than deserve a free coffee after the hell you've been put through this week.

"You have no idea," she said, rolling her eyes. "Is Dan talking to you?"

"Outside of the gym, no," Zach said, taking the lid off his coffee to let it cool. "He's kind of been a jerk since this past spring anyway though, so I don't really think it's much of a loss. Ever since Coach made him the starting pitcher last season, he thinks he's better than everyone else."

"Tell me about it," Ariana said. Zach said nothing. He saw Ariana rub her eye and cringed.

"Do you want to know why I invited you here today?" he asked.

"Because you feel sorry for me?"

"No. I think you deserve to know the truth. Or at least what I think is the truth."

Ariana met his gaze. His green eyes seemed sincere, so she nodded to signal that she was ready to hear it.

"I think the reason I started dancing with you on Friday was because in my head, you weren't taken. See, the way Dan talks about you, well, it's like the way he talks about every other girl. He'd talk about you and Marcy in the same breath, as if there wasn't a difference."

Zach watched Ariana's face contort in pain and quickly corrected himself.

"I'm sorry, I didn't mean it like that. I- I don't know what I'm trying to say."

Zach shook his head and Ariana inhaled sharply to hold back her tears.

Zach sighed and considered his words before beginning again.

"The baseball team has this thing that whatever happens on the field stays on the field. Or in the case of the current off-season, the gym. Anyway, that's usually supposed to refer to people giving their all to the game, but sometimes it includes more personal things. A couple weeks ago, Dan mentioned that he'd been studying with Marcy and kind of implied that something more was going on. That was one of the things we kept on the field, but now I realize how messed up that was. I should have told you. I'm sorry."

Ariana's face fell and she wanted to cry again. She gulped, and looked into Zach's green eyes, which also looked glassy with tears.

"Even then, he didn't flat out admit it to anyone," she said. "And why would you have told me? No offense or anything, but we weren't exactly friends."

"None taken. Are you okay?"

"Eh, okay is pretty subjective. I finally have proof that Dan and Marcy were flirting while we were dating, so I feel less paranoid and crazy. But at the same time, he was clearly cheating in some capacity so that makes me feel like shit because everyone thinks that I cheated on him." Ariana took a small sip of her coffee.

"Yeah, I mean, we shouldn't have done what we did but he wasn't exactly innocent himself if that makes you feel better. Honestly, I don't know why everyone is talking about you and my name hasn't come up once. Sure, the entire baseball team knows it was me, but other than that, most people don't. And they don't seem to care to find out who it was you slept with, which is bizarre."

"No, it's not," Ariana said, her head down, "They don't care 'cause it's a double standard. It's the whole, 'men are biologically programmed to have sex with everyone' thing. They don't care about a guy sleeping around because it's 'normal'."

"Well I don't think I'm exactly in a position to advocate for feminism," he said, sitting upright, "but I can advocate for you," He laid a hand gently on her forearm and she looked up at him.

"And how on earth do you plan to do that?"

"For one thing, I can tell everyone that Dan was cheating on you with Marcy. That will take some of the focus off you and maybe even make what we did look justifiable."

Ariana mused on the thought of spreading rumors about Dan, but had a feeling that somehow, he'd find a way to turn it around on her and make her look like the bad guy. After all, when she had confronted him about forming a study group, he had blamed her for not proactively texting both him and Marcy weeks in advance.

"That's okay," she said, "you don't have to do that. He'll just find a way to turn it back on me."

"Then how can I help?" Zach asked. He looked genuinely concerned and Ariana felt warm and fuzzy inside for the first time in a while.

"I could really use a friend right now," she said.

17

Sweat and Tears

Nancy was still trying to process Frank's reaction when she went to her third personal training session on Monday. She was beginning to wonder if something had happened. *Maybe his father is distracting him*, she thought. She met her trainer in the lobby of the gym and they headed towards the treadmills and ellipticals after exchanging pleasantries. Nancy looked towards the treadmill with dread but glanced down at her body and reminded herself why she was there.

"Okay, I know I had you do half a mile for a warm up last time. Today, let's try for a whole mile."

"I don't know if I can," Nancy said. She had struggled to get through her warm up last time and had wanted to vomit afterwards.

"Go slow," her trainer responded, "it's not a race."

"Okay," Nancy said, stepping up onto the machine.

She turned it on and set herself at a moderate pace. Within the first quarter mile, she felt her heart rate skyrocket, but pushed through it. *One quarter of the way there,* she thought. She hadn't run much even when she was in shape because she was awful at it, so using the treadmill as a warm up felt like a cruel and unusual punishment.

"Can I switch to the bike?" Nancy asked at the half mile mark.

"We're going to do that later," her trainer said. "You're half way there though."

Nancy didn't reply, partly because she was annoyed and partly because she was breathing too hard. She found herself mentally cursing out her trainer, but as she glanced over and saw her running on the treadmill next to her, she stopped. It wasn't her trainer's fault that Nancy was out of shape. She wasn't asking a lot of her. She could have run a mile when she was in shape. She might not have been the fastest, but she knew she wouldn't have struggled this much. Twelve minutes later, Nancy finished her mile and stepped off the treadmill. Her trainer followed suit and led her towards the weight machines. Nancy glanced at the trainer's treadmill as she passed to see that she had run two miles in the time it had taken her to run one. As she began her weight work out, she felt defeated. Her first two sessions hadn't seemed so hard because the trainer had been trying to find her limits. Now she was trying to push them and Nancy wondered if they could ever be overcome.

18

The Funeral

They had the funeral the day before Thanksgiving. Lisa wore a long-sleeved black dress with a black veiled hat and Frank wore the same suit he'd been wearing to court since he became a lawyer. They sat on opposite ends of the small chapel, surrounded by a small number of extended family and some of Lisa's friends. Lisa's husband sat next to her and held her hand during the service. Her daughter, who was only four, sat next to her, unable to comprehend what was happening beyond knowing that she was supposed to be quiet and well-behaved. Frank glanced over at the mourning family, viewing them as subjects in a painting. He thought that maybe if he was looking at them in a museum, he might want to get to know the little girl. Then he glanced towards Lisa and remembered why he hadn't met his one and only niece.

His sister had shut him out when she was a teenager and when he was just starting his career. She had decided one day that she hated her brother and hadn't stopped hating him since. Frank knew that he had probably instigated her hatred for him on some level but didn't know how to fix the problem and didn't care to figure it out. He had always been jealous of her because his parents had been nicer to her when she was growing up than they had been to him. It was easy for him to channel that jealousy back into reciprocated hate for his sister who got coddled compared to him. Whenever she would harass him for not visiting their father enough, he used to tell her that the father she grew up with and the father he grew up with were two different people. She wasn't there for the financial stress and her father's angry outbursts at Frank for not being good enough. By the time she was growing up, their father was doing better financially and was consistently paying the bills on time. Frank had convinced himself that she wouldn't understand his days sitting in their cold and dark basement, eating baked beans out of a can.

Lisa rose to read her eulogy and Frank rolled his eyes, wishing he had had her childhood. *If I was a girl, I bet he wouldn't have been so hard on me. But they were also older when they had her, so maybe they got softer with age, too. Damn it, she actually had parents.*

Lisa broke down into uncontrollable sobs in her

last few lines and her husband stood up and gently escorted her off the stage. The priest closed the ceremony and everyone filtered out of the church and into their respective limos.

The reception was held at a quaint Italian restaurant with a small courtyard outside. The courtyard housed four concrete benches that surrounded a small fountain. Tulips and daisies were planted around the perimeter of the fountain and lined the small paved path that connected the restaurant to the courtyard. Frank thought the flowers looked pretty, but found the pairing quite odd. He paced around the perimeter of the courtyard with a glass of scotch in his hand and stared at the female statue holding the bowl the fountain water was pouring out of on top of her head. He focused in on her expression, trying to figure out if she was happy to be a water bearer, or if she was just doing it because she was molded that way.

Footsteps interrupted his train of thought and he looked up to see his sister approaching him. He half raised the hand he was holding his scotch in to acknowledge her before taking another sip.

"Listen, I know you're probably still mad at me, but I did what I thought was right. He would have died last week if he hadn't gone on the blood thinner."

"Whatever," Frank said, looking down and

swirling his scotch.

"I'm sorry," Lisa said, tears beginning to well up in her red eyes. Her face was splotchy from crying all day and Frank realized that he had barely shed a tear. He looked away and took a few steps, trying to make himself cry. He managed to get a small tear to drip out of his left eye and turned back around.

"He was miserable anyway," he said. Lisa's tears slowly traveled down her cheeks but she stopped crying momentarily.

"Yeah, he was," she agreed. She had taken her hat off and the breeze wisped her hair in all different directions. "Can we just put this behind us? Can we start fresh?"

"I don't know," Frank said, taking another sip of his scotch.

"Dad never liked seeing us fight," she said, wiping another tear. She looked around as if something was missing.

"Wait, where are Nancy and the kids?"

Frank deflated. For the past forty-eight hours, he had forgotten that his family existed.

"Nancy and I are getting a divorce," he said, finishing off his scotch.

"What? When did this happen?"

"I don't know. About a week ago, I think."

"I'm sorry," Lisa said, hugging him. He half hugged her back and she pulled away.

"Wait, that explains Nancy but why aren't the kids here?"

"I didn't want to upset them this close to the holidays. I'll tell them after," he half lied. In reality, he didn't think his kids deserved to know that their grandfather had died. They had rarely accompanied him when he visited his father and he didn't think it was their loss to mourn.

Lisa broke the silence that was beginning to set in. "Why don't you come over for Thanksgiving tomorrow? It was just going to be me and Jack anyway. You can meet Galina." She gave him a soft smile and walked back into the restaurant.

19

Giving Thanks

Nancy woke up alone in her bed on Thanksgiving, *Oh great, now I get to face my mother's judgment*, she said. She pulled the sheets up over her head as if she could shield herself from the world. She lay in bed for ten minutes until the cat started rubbing up against her leg and meowing for breakfast. She grudgingly got up and followed the cat down stairs to the main level and then down another flight to the basement. She opened a can onto a plate in the corner of the basement, listening to him purr as he ate for a moment. She went upstairs to the main level and rinsed the cat food can off in the sink. She went to the fridge and started cutting up some strawberries. She then grabbed some blueberries and quickly washed them. Finally, she grabbed some yogurt and granola and began assembling little parfaits in wine glasses. Once they were done, she set them in the fridge and then went upstairs to wake up Ariana and Teddy.

"Let's go, we need to be at Grandma's for noon! We have an hour and a half to get ready."

Ariana and Teddy both slowly rolled out of bed and began getting ready. As Teddy looked in the mirror for the first time that morning, he realized just how badly he was in need of a shave. He had just thrown his old blade out and opened the bathroom cabinets to search for a new one. When he couldn't find one in the three places he might have put it, he instinctively yelled, "Dad, can I borrow your razor?"

Nancy, who was curling her hair in her bathroom, gulped.

"Dad?" Teddy tried again, walking down the hall and towards the master bedroom. He peeked into his mom's bathroom.

"He's been spending the past week at Andy's," Nancy said, looking at herself in the mirror and avoiding Teddy's eyes.

"Crap, I'm sorry, Mom. I'm still half asleep."

Nancy sighed.

"It's okay." She released the curling iron from her head, revealing a cascading curl and grabbed another piece of hair. "It feels weird for me too."

"I'm sorry," he began, "are you okay?"

Nancy took a deep breath in and felt a pang in her chest. "No. I haven't been okay for a while," she said, relieved that she was finally being honest with someone about how she had been feeling.

"Are you guys going through with the divorce?"

"Yes," Nancy said, putting her curling iron down on her bathroom vanity and fluffing her auburn curls.

"And you're okay with that?" Teddy said.

"I think so," Nancy said, surprising herself as well as her son. She had been trying to cope with change better and felt that even though it was terrifying, in this case, it was for the best.

* * *

All three of them breathed a huge sigh on their way home from Thanksgiving. Ariana was glad that nobody remembered that she had had a boyfriend and was able to escape the day without thinking too much about Dan. Even when he did pop into her mind, it wasn't in an emotional or romantic way but in a way that just reminded her of his existence.

Teddy was busy trying to recall the number of glasses of wine he had. He had never really gotten drunk at a family gathering before, but had found himself bored and looking for entertainment. He had found it in the form of wine and talking politics with one of his uncles. It had been entertaining because it had been about two years since either of them had actually bothered to watch or read the news. They went on and on about the way the world used to be like a bunch of old men even though his uncle was only forty-one. They had laughed about the ridiculous things they had heard other people talking about when they spoke of Donald Trump. Teddy reveled in the laughter, in having a real conversation for the first time in a while. He had been surprised to find that his uncle wasn't nearly as judgmental as some of his mother's other family members were.

Nancy was simply relieved to be heading home and away from the strange creature that was her mother. When she had told her mother about Frank, she had expected her to say, "I told you so," and "He was a bad egg from the start" and cringed when her mother actually said those things at the table. What she hadn't expected was for her mother to say that it would be a good thing if they got divorced. Nancy was grateful that her mother had enough tact to say that to her when they were alone in the kitchen, but felt wary of it.

"Honey, sometimes you just can't make things work regardless of how hard you try. Some things just weren't meant to be."

"I thought you thought divorce was a cop out," Nancy had said.

"In most cases it is," she had said, nodding, "but in some cases, it's survival." She had looked at her daughter and pointed to her stomach.

"This is him," she had said, "consuming you alive. You were always a stick until him," she said, holding her index finger up to emphasize her point.

Those words reverberated through Nancy on the drive home. She had protested that it wasn't him, it was her injury, but her mother had made her question herself. *Maybe if I hadn't been so stressed and unhappy, I wouldn't have eaten so much and stopped moving. Maybe he paralyzed me,* she thought.

* * *

Frank's Thanksgiving didn't go as smoothly. His brother-in-law scoffed when he walked through the door and he sensed that even the four-year-old niece he had never met already disliked him. As Lisa finished preparing the meal, he found himself stuck on the sofa with his brother-in-law, Jack, who was engrossed in the football game on TV. Frank pretended to watch the game, but found himself instead watching Galina play with her dolls on the floor in front of the TV. He remembered when Ariana used to play with her dolls and was reminded of how much had changed since then. He felt a strange aching, but he knew it was too late. He had too much pride and not enough time to rebuild any of the relationships he had ruined.

Lisa interrupted them from the game and both men got up and made their way to the dining room, followed by Galina. They all sat down at the table and Lisa said grace, making sure to be thankful that her brother was there. Frank gave her a small smile before they all said "Amen". They made small talk about the food for a while, Jack complimenting Lisa on her mashed potatoes and Frank marveling at how much food she had made. Suddenly, Lisa changed the topic.

"I'm sorry about you and Nancy," she said to Frank. "How are the kids taking it?"

"I don't know," he said, mushing his cranberry sauce with his fork, "I haven't talked to them since I left."

"Well you're going to, right?" Jack interjected.

"I don't know," Frank said, lifting a forkful of lumpy cranberry sauce to his mouth, "They hate me."

"You're still their father though," Lisa said.

Frank swallowed and wiped his mouth.

"I don't think that means as much as you think it does," he said.

"Well you and Dad didn't have the best relationship and you still visited him in the home," she said, sipping her wine.

"Yeah, but that was different," Frank said, thinking of all the awful things he had said to his father once he had graduated law school and finally moved out. They had never talked about much more than the weather after that despite Yosyp's weekly calls to Frank. "Can we talk about something else?"

20

Christmas Eve

Ariana sat at her desk drawing check marks next to the names of people she had bought Christmas presents for. She had checked off, her mother, Teddy, Kelsey, and her grandmother, and placed a question mark next to her father. When she got bored of trying to remember if she had forgotten anyone, she moved her list to the right side of her desk and grabbed her journal. She hadn't written in it since before Thanksgiving and re-read over what she had written previously.

Why is this so confusing? I think I may be developing a crush on Zach. We only met up a couple times but every time he texts, I get butterflies. I can't even remember having sex with him either, so I'm curious as to what it was like. Maybe I enjoyed it. Maybe he remembers it and he enjoyed it too. Maybe that's why he's talking to me, but he definitely respects me enough not to mention it if that's the case.

He's just so sweet. He texted me the other day out of the blue, saying, "I know you're working through some stuff, but just remember that I'm here if you need a friend." I wish Kelsey would do that. I don't think she means anything by not doing it though. I just don't think she knows what it means to be a friend.

I remember Dan making comments about Zach sleeping around the school as if that made him a bad person, but now I'm not so sure it does. The more I talk with him, the more I realize how honest he is. I even did my own little research project and mentioned his name to some of the girls who I know have been involved with him. They never had anything bad to say about him, so I'm guessing Dan was just jealous.

I remember when Dan and I used to get milkshakes together at the diner downtown. We would always start talking about the stupidest things and end up having some existential conversation. He gave me my first kiss at that diner, right after we wrapped up our discussion of religion and science. He had told me that I was more beautiful than I could ever know and leaned in to kiss me. I miss that innocence. I wonder if I'll ever truly be able to experience that again, especially with Zach.

Ariana grabbed a pen from her desk organizer and flipped onto a fresh page.

I need to put Dan in my past. Yes, it's aggravating that it ended the way it did, but it's holding me back. I need to focus on the future, on my potential career. I just got an early acceptance letter from Brandeis so I'm excited to start looking into their psych program.

<u>2019 Resolutions</u>
Research different majors/ psych careers
Forgive myself
Let things go
Reclaim my GPA
Journal more often
Start a blog?

"Ariana!" her mother interrupted. She had just picked up her pen to jot down another New Year's resolution.

"What?" Ariana called back.

"I need your help with these lights."

"Okay, I'm coming," Ariana said, closing her journal with a heavy sigh. She got up and headed down the stairs. She turned the corner to the living room and saw her mom hanging Christmas lights on the mantle. Nancy taped the string of lights down and turned around to face Ariana, who was looking around the room. Nancy had covered the room in wreaths of all colors and sizes and had set a nativity scene up next to the Christmas tree. She had placed the Biblical figurines on fake snow and Ariana marveled at all the decorations.

"Wow, you've been busy," she said.

"It looks good, doesn't it?"

"Yeah," Ariana said, "very festive." *Oh my God, it looks like the Christmas Tree Shop exploded,* she thought. "Do you need help with those lights?" she asked, motioning towards the mantle.

"Oh no, honey, I need help with these," she said, picking up a pile of lights at her feet. She had lost about fifteen pounds since she had started working out in early November and moving around the house was beginning to seem easier.

"Where are they going?"

"In the attic," Nancy said, handing them off to her and motioning upstairs.

"Okay," Ariana said, turning around and heading back upstairs.

Nancy finished fiddling with the lights on the mantle, took a deep breath, and sat down on the couch to admire her work. She never used to decorate much because Frank felt decorations were an unnecessary waste of space and money. She felt tears begin to form as she stared at her wreaths but found herself smiling as well. She knew that this Christmas was going to be different. She told her children that they should text their father to arrange a get together either tonight or tomorrow but she wasn't sure if they had done so. *You can't force them to have a relationship,* she reminded herself as Ariana came back downstairs empty handed. Nancy secretly wished that their relationship with their father would slowly erode over time so that she could completely erase Frank from her life but felt it was necessary to put on a facade, at least around the holidays.

"Did you get a chance to text Dad?" Nancy asked, slowly lifting herself from the couch.

"No," Ariana said, looking down and heading into the kitchen. She opened the fridge, grabbed a plate of grapes and sat down at the kitchen table so that she was facing her mom. Nancy walked over and pulled up the seat across from her daughter.

"I know you and your brother don't have the best relationship with him," Nancy began, grabbing a grape from the plate, "but I think it would mean a lot to him if you guys reached out."

"Mom," Ariana said, holding a grape mid-air, "he hasn't reached out to us in over a month. You really think it would mean a lot?"

Nancy shifted in her seat. "Your father has a lot of pride," she said, reaching for a grape. "You need to be the one to reach out to him."

"My father doesn't know how to be a real man," she muttered, pulling her phone out of her pocket and sending her dad a quick text to appease her mom.

"Happy?" she asked Nancy. She pushed the plate of grapes towards her mom, stood up, and walked away.

* * *

Teddy came home around seven in his Fed-Ex uniform. He pushed his bangs off his forehead to cool down, but that didn't seem to help. He saw his mother checking something in the oven and went upstairs to shower. The house smelled like ham and he found his mouth watering as he washed the day off of him.

He didn't dislike his job, but he got tired of the monotony. He knew he couldn't complain though because they hadn't asked him for a drug test yet unlike most of the companies he had applied to. He hadn't smoked in almost a month but knew that he was far from in the clear as far as drug testing was concerned. Every time he wanted to call Dexter just for the sake of smoking, he tried to remind himself that if he wanted a job, he needed to hold off, at least for the time being. As he washed his back, he found himself laughing at Dexter's reaction when he asked him to play basketball the other day.

"When did we become jocks?" Dexter had asked as Teddy dribbled down the court towards him.

"Since I'm working on trying to get a real job," Teddy said. He took a hard right and blew past Dexter. Dexter ran to catch up and blocked him just as he went to shoot. The ball went past Teddy and he ran after it.

"That's good for you man, but don't go making me run any marathons with you."

Teddy retrieved the ball and laughed as he turned around and dribbled back towards Dexter. "Don't worry, I'm allergic to running. That and soccer."

Teddy finished his shower and turned off the water. He dried himself and slipped his clothes on. He thought he heard the garage door and slightly opened the bathroom door as he was cleaning his ears out with a Q-Tip. He heard an unfamiliar woman's voice and then his dad's. He shut his bathroom door and grabbed the vanity for support.

"Motherfucker!" he harshly whispered. He feared that the woman was his father's new girlfriend and took his time blow drying and combing his hair, trying to avoid the inevitable interaction for as long as possible. He walked over towards Ariana's room and knocked on the door. He was met with silence, and figured she was already trapped downstairs with his father and his new bimbo. *I guess I should go save her,* he thought to himself as he ran gel through his hair. He checked himself out in the mirror and went downstairs.

He found his dad, sister, mother, and Aunt Lisa all at the table, talking and laughing. He breathed a sigh of relief upon realizing that the woman he had heard from upstairs wasn't his dad's new girlfriend. He hugged his aunt and they exchanged happy "hello's". His eyes widened when he got closer and saw all the food his mother had set up on the counter. He could see the ham poking up over the edge of the aluminum tray it was contained in and began to wonder what was in the other four trays.

"Hey Teddy," Nancy said, "we were just waiting for you to start eating. Why don't you make a plate? There are folding chairs in the hallway that you can pull up."

"Okay," Teddy said, heading to the hallway to grab a couple chairs. He was beginning to wonder why his mother had invited his father and his aunt over. He knew it was Christmas Eve, but it still seemed strange, especially because he hadn't seen his aunt since he was a little kid. He brought the folding chairs over to the table and waited for his family to finish serving themselves before heading over to the counter and serving himself. He was thrilled to find eggplant parmigiana, roasted potatoes, and sausage and peppers alongside the ham and he filled his plate with a little bit of everything. He walked back to the corner of the table he had claimed between Ariana and his mother and sat down to eat.

"So Lisa, where's Jack and Galina?" Nancy asked.

"They're actually at Jack's parents. They do Christmas Eve with them every year."

"Aww that's nice. Well, I'm glad to hear that you and Frank are talking again. May I ask what happened?" she asked, casting Frank a suspicious sideways glance.

"Well, we kind of reconnected at the funeral," Lisa said, resting her hand on Frank's forearm. "We knew Dad wouldn't want us to keep living the way we were."

Ariana and Teddy looked up and dropped their forks.

"Grandpa died?" Ariana asked. Lisa pulled her hand away and shot an angry and bewildered look at Frank.

"You didn't tell them?" Lisa said through gritted teeth at a volume that only Frank could hear.

Nancy, who was equally shocked, turned red in the face and looked as though she was about to say something. She quickly shoved another forkful of eggplant into her mouth to prevent herself from bursting out with anger at Frank for not having told her or the kids.

"Dad, why wouldn't you tell us something like that?" Teddy cut in.

Frank's face flushed when he saw how angry and sad his kids were. He knew he needed to say something, but wasn't sure what. "I didn't want to upset you," he lied. He knew that if he had said the truth, which was that he thought it was none of their business, both his sister and his ex-wife would jump down his throat.

"We have a right to know that kind of stuff, Dad," Ariana said sternly. "After all, he was our grandfather."

"It was right around the time your mother and I had just separated and I didn't want to upset you further," he lied again. He was impressed by how good his lie sounded out loud and smiled a little bit. He quickly caught himself and made himself appear somber again.

Teddy could feel his anger coursing through his veins and balled his fists together under the table. "And when were you going to tell us Dad? On Christmas, when one of us asked who's going to the home to see him? Or were you going to lie then too? God, I'm glad I didn't do well in school because I never want to be a lawyer like you. All you do all day is lie and congratu-fucking-lations, you're tearing your family apart because you don't know the truth anymore." Teddy stood up. He was shaking with rage and it took every fiber of his being to hold himself back from reaching across the table and punching his dad in the face. "If you bought me a present, return it." He stormed off, stomping up the stairs.

"You can return my gift too," Ariana said, standing up with her plate in hand. "I can't believe I let Mom convince me to give you a second chance." She grabbed Teddy's plate in her other hand and carried their food upstairs. She knocked on Teddy's door with her elbow. "It's me," she said when her knock was met with silence. Teddy slowly opened the door. "I figure you're still hungry," she said, "can I come in?"

* * *

Lisa and Nancy were both livid. "Are you kidding me?" they said in unison, Lisa practically throwing her chair back as she stood up. Frank sat there, stunned. He hadn't expected to walk into this argument and hadn't thought up counterarguments.

"I let you back in my life, feeling sorry that your kids and wife have abandoned you, and the reason you're all alone is because you're the one pushing them away with all your lies? I should have known you weren't telling the truth. Do you get high off of this, this manipulation? What kind of father doesn't tell his kids their grandfather died? Were you ever going to tell them?"

"Eventually," Frank half lied. He hadn't expected a text from his daughter and had considered telling her for a split second before he decided for the second time that it wasn't her business.

Nancy stood up slowly and brought her plate to the sink. Any hesitation she had felt about the divorce had now melted away. Unable to manage more words through her rage, Lisa grabbed her plate and followed Nancy. Nancy turned around to voice some choice words but Lisa beat her to the punch.

"You're a sad excuse for a man," she screamed. "What the hell is wrong with you? You know, don't answer that, I know what's wrong with you. You're a fucking asshole and you always will be. I'm leaving," she said, pulling her keys out of her pocket.

"Lisa, wait," he said, standing up and putting his hands together pleadingly.

"No, I'm not waiting. Call an Uber and find a room. I can't be near you right now." She hurriedly pulled on her coat which was hanging in a nearby closet and threw her purse over her shoulder.

"I've given you so many chances Frank. You've never treated me like a sister," she continued, pulling her gloves on.

"Merry Christmas," she said to Nancy, giving her a quick hug. "Tell the kids Merry Christmas for me too. Their presents are in this bag," she said, motioning towards a large Target bag by the basement door. She slammed the door and Frank turned around to glance at Nancy.

Seeing the livid expression on Nancy's face, Frank quickly shrugged his coat on and called a car. He watched the snow fall as his Uber driver listened to Trans-Siberian Orchestra's rendition of "Joy to the World" and, unamused by the irony, slammed his hand on the side of the car door. He had no one to play the role of wife, daughter, son, or sister, and for the first time, he felt lost. But as he watched the snow fall and realized that it filled the alleys between buildings, bridging the gap, he realized would find other people to play these roles, to fill the gaps between his night and day.

* * *

They sat cross-legged on the floor as they ate and listened to the fight die down downstairs. "I'm sorry," Ariana began, "Mom told me to text Dad and give him another chance but she was wrong. I shouldn't have bothered."

"It's not your fault," he said. "For all you know, he could have changed into a decent person in the past month."

"I guess, but people don't really change."

"I like to think that I'm changing," Teddy said.

"Yeah, but you're making an active effort," Ariana said, brushing her hair back behind her right ear. She poked at a potato with her fork. "Most people don't want to do that. Hell, I don't think Dad's realized that he needs to change. The man lied to us about our grandfather dying for Christ's sake.

"True. Change requires a conscious effort. At least he's talking to Aunt Lisa again."

Ariana snorted. "For how long? She might have thought he changed but she looked horrified when she realized he didn't tell us about Grandpa. Also, did you not hear that screaming five minutes ago? I don't think it went well down there."

Teddy nodded in agreement and ate some more of his food. "Let's promise to never be like them," he said. "You know, to be honest with each other."

Ariana chewed her food thoughtfully. She could hear her Aunt's engine revving outside. "We'll never be like them," she said, smiling sadly.

"Okay," he said, "so what's really going on in your life?"

Ariana took a deep breath, trying to figure out where her story began and wondering how it would end.

Afterword

When I first started writing about Ariana and Teddy during my freshman year of college, I didn't know much about either of them. Their personalities seemed to escape me and my instinct was to put them in awful situations (a violent rape for Ariana and a severe drug addiction for Teddy) to mask the fact that I didn't really know who they were. It was through a fiction workshop during my senior year of college that my classmates and professor, Clark Knowles, reigned me in from my extreme plot elements. They also asked me where their parents were, which is when Clark recommended writing outside the story to discover what was going on behind the scenes. Suddenly the characters of Nancy and Frank emerged with their own unique problems, and the classic suburban white picket fence family became the basis of my story.

When I handed in my final short story for Clark's class, it was about 40 pages long. Clark sent me his feedback on it the summer after I graduated, so I did what any writer is supposed to do: I read it and then put it in a drawer for about a month as I worked and looked for a new job. When my job search wasn't fruitful, I gave up and opened the drawer. Clark thought that I still had more story to tell, so I decided to tell it. It felt a lot more rewarding than the radio silence I was receiving from sending out my resume and cover letter. The thought of working on my novel before work was sometimes the only thing that got me out of bed in the morning.

Acknowledgements

First and foremost, I would like to thank my parents, Deborah Kiefer and John McKeown, for instilling a strong work ethic in me and supporting me through this process. I would also like to thank all my friends and family who supported me along the way. Because I eventually decided to self-publish, some of them weren't just my support system, but my team of editors. This book would not have been possible without my team of readers, Cristina Mancini, Kellie Reardon, Angela Matijczak, Laura Szamatulski, and Christine Pond, all of whom read each draft I sent them and provided feedback. I would also like to thank Adam Cebulski, Dalton Wilbur, and Jessica Konkol for reading through the manuscript before it went to press. Lastly, I owe a huge thank you to Brittney Leach for designing the beautiful cover.

Because this is my first novel, I would be remiss if I didn't thank all the teachers and professors who helped me along the way. Sean Kienle, Keri Heverling, Ann Williams, Monica Chiu, and Diane Freedman all offered their unique writing lessons and were sources of inspiration when my faith was scarce. Last but not least, I owe a huge thank you to Clark Knowles, who told me the importance of writing outside the story. I don't know if either of us knew that the short story I brought to him three years ago had the potential to become a novel, but I do know that this novel wouldn't have been possible without his feedback and guidance.

www.ingramcontent.com/pod-product-compliance
Lightning Source LLC
LaVergne TN
LVHW041700060526
838201LV00043B/512